SPELLCRACKER'S HONEYMOON

TANSY RAYNER ROBERTS

ISBN: 978-0-6488983-2-0 (ebook)

ISBN: 978-0-6488983-3-7 (paperback)

❀ Created with Vellum

For Harriet, who knew how to honeymoon
And Sarah, who knew how to rock a masquerade

CONTENTS

DRAMATIS PERSONAE

MRS MNEMOSYNE "MNEME" SEABOURNE, *a respectably married young lady*

MR C. THORNBURY SEABOURNE, *a spellcracker of note who enjoys long walks*

QUEEN AUD, *monarch of the Teacup Isles*

ALFRED, LORD MANTICORE, *the Queen's Advisor on Magical Matters; a terribly important gentleman*

LADY PERSIMMON MANTICORE, *a troubled wife*

MISS THISBE WHEATEN, *reporter for The Gentlewoman, a popular ladies magazine*

FREDDIE, ALFIE AND ED, *a cluster of rapscallions*

MRS ELECTRA CHESHIRE, *a social secretary*

MR OCTAVIAN SWIFT, QUEEN'S CONSULTANT, *secret spymaster and father*

MRS PHOEBE HOLIDAY, *a friendly young matron*

DETECTIVE INSPECTOR GORDON HOLIDAY, *a working husband*

GREAT AUNT EDITH, *a social-climbing relative*

HENRY, DUKE OF STORM, *a dear cousin and retired secret agent*

JUNO, DUCHESS OF STORM, *a dear friend and ballroom expert*

MR EDMUND CHESHIRE, *a deceased husband*

KING OSBERT, *a deceased king, great-grandfather to Queen Aud, not appearing in this story*

MRS DR LETTY ST SWITHINS, *a dear friend and correspondent*

LADY LIESL OF SANDWICH, *a dear friend and correspondent*

MISS METIS SEABOURNE, *a dear cousin and most unsatisfactory correspondent*

ASSORTED NURSEMAIDS, AND A BABY.

CORRESPONDENCE FROM A
HONEYMOON

FROM: *MRS MNEMOSYNE SEABOURNE, COMFREY
COTTAGE, MUDGELY, THE ISLE OF ASTER*

TO: *MRS DR ST SWITHINS, GLEN LETHE, THE
ISLE OF MEMORY.*

*M*y dear Letty,
              I am so sorry that I did not get more of
a chance to speak with you at the reception. What a whirl
it was! I am on the whole glad that we did not choose to
elope entirely, though Mr Thornbury clearly had a plan up
his sleeve to offer this alternative up until the very last
moment.

Mr Seabourne, I should say! That will take quite a bit
of getting used to, I can tell you. Luckily for me, my
husband is not especially fond of his proper name, and so
he intends to go by C. Thornbury Seabourne in public,

and will reserve 'Thornbury' for most intimate acquaintances. Including, of course, his wife.

It was a splendid day, though my family's recent history
with weddings does rather mean that it counts as successful
as long as no one has attempted to hex the groom, or
throw hedgehogs in the temple. My mother will, I imagine,
never entirely forgive me for providing Bath buns and
elderflower ices for our guests instead of wedding cake, but
she cannot say a word about it given the events of, well,
you know very well to what I am referring.

(Any bride who has ever had to rescue her future
husband from being suffocated inside a wedding cake has,
I rather feel, complete license to avoid ordering a marzipan
monstrosity for herself.)

In any case, I survived the wedding without more
drama than is to be expected for a Seabourne, and set sail
with my husband on our honeymoon.

I say set sail, though our travel took almost no time at
all thanks to the joyous magical revolution concerning
portals. My husband had a final joke to play on me,
however, as the quiet and reclusive holiday he arranged for
us turned out to be near the lakeside village of Mudgely on
the Isle of Aster, of all places.

But my dear Mnemosyne, I hear you ask, isn't the Isle
of Aster completely devoid of magic, and thus the only
one of the Teacup Isles to be completely inaccessible by
portal travel?

Why yes, my sweet, IT IS TRUE. At one point, he said
to me with a completely straight face that he knew of my
deep love for swan-shaped boats and he did not want to
deprive me of the experience.

Then, just as I was on the verge of transforming him
into the world's largest teacup, he revealed that in fact
there was a bridge between Aster and the Isle of Manti-

core, which is extremely accessible by portal travel of all kinds.

My husband the jester, who would have thought it?

In any case, I have avoided all feathery modes of water transportation and am now ensconced quite snug in the dearest of cottages (generously sized enough that it might be considered a very small country manor house), for an entire month (honeymoon indeed!) of wifely amusements.

Try not to miss me too much. I will not, I fear, think of you at all.

Your beloved friend,

Mrs Mnemosyne Seabourne

PS: Thank you for taking care of Basil while I am away, please remember not to let him near any cutlery as he has an unfortunate habit of eating it and it does terrible things to his digestion.

❧

WIFE,

Fear not. I have taken a stroll to the farm over the hill. No one has been kidnapped by pirates. I shall return with breakfast eggs and milk.

Yours,

C. Thornbury S.

❧

HUSBAND,

Fear not. I have retired to the upstairs parlour to read a book that caught my eye upon our first tour of the house. No one has been eaten by ghosts. I prefer my eggs with a dab of mustard, a surfeit of black pepper, and three slices of toast.

Yours,
Mrs. S.

∾

FROM: *C. THORNBURY SEABOURNE, COMFREY COTTAGE, MUDGELY, THE ISLE OF ASTER*

TO: *THE DUKE OF STORM, STORM BOLT, THE ISLE OF TOWN*

M**Y** **DEAR** **FELLOW**,

We have arrived safely as I'm sure you are aware from your contacts. While it is true that we shall be out of magical contact for the duration, we are certainly well protected. Do not worry yourself.

Also, please do not accept that appointment with the Earl of Sandwich and his son until I am back in Town and able to aid in all diplomatic relations. Viscount Gustav has never quite forgiven you for choosing not to marry his sister, and I do not want to read in a newspaper that you have been killed in a duel, or that your nose has been charmed to resemble a spotted aardvark (again).

Mneme sends her love and has enclosed a letter for Juno.

Regards,
C. Thornbury Seabourne, Esquire

∾

TO: THE DUCHESS OF STORM, STORM BOLT, THE
ISLE OF TOWN

MY DARLING JUNO,

My new husband is a maniac.

It seemed such a clever idea of his, to honeymoon here
on the beautiful magic-free island of Aster. If it's good
enough for her Majesty the Queen, after all…

But splendid views and cozy cottages notwithstanding,
my darling husband when deprived of magic and other
forms of work transforms into an utter beast for fresh air
and exercise.

Every day he is out there, marching up and down hills,
hiking across tarns, and taking great lungfuls of fresh air as
if he had never seen an island before. I don't know what to
make of it, but my greater distress is how often he wishes
me to join him.

Do not mistake me: I love my husband dearly and
would gladly spend this honey-month entirely in his presence. But must I climb a mountain every day to share his
company? My hair is quite out of sorts from so much
exposure to brisk breezes and sunshine, and I have at least
fourteen more freckles than I did before leaving our
wedding reception.

I hope you and Henry are well, and that the pleasing
news you confided to me over buns last week causes you no
particular discomfort.

Do not read my letter to your husband!

Your beloved friend,

Mneme

❧

FROM: *MRS MNEMOSYNE SEABOURNE, COMFREY COTTAGE, MUDGELY, THE ISLE OF ASTER*

TO: *MISS METIS SEABOURNE, LOCATION UNKNOWN, THE CONTINENT*

MY DEAREST COUSIN,

I hope this letter finds you well — indeed, that it finds you at all. Diplomatic channels are supposed to be efficient at locating stray members of the nobility while they partake in Grand Tours on the Continent. Clearly, something went wrong with the system, as all three of the wedding invitations I sent you must have gone astray.

Please send me a note when you can to let me know you are well. That no more disasters, familial or otherwise, have occurred. The controversy over our family scandal has died down somewhat over the last few months, and I think you would find it very agreeable to attempt another Season very soon, especially with two respectably married Seabourne cousins to ensure as many invitations as you wish (well, one respectably married Duke and one very quietly respectable cousin with friends in high places, but you know what I mean).

Your mamma was not invited to my wedding, nor did she send a note of congratulation, though I know that my own mamma visits her regularly in her confinement, so you can be sure that her needs are attended to.

It was a most pleasant wedding. I felt your absence keenly. Please do send word. I am honeymooning for a month on the Isle of Aster, where no magical communication is possible, but you can send a letter by special messenger — or charm a note home to the Seabourne estate, or to Cousin Henry at Storm Bolt, which will be passed on to me with all due efficiency.

Please, Metis. We worry so about you.

Your beloved cousin,

Mneme

~

WIFE,

As you know, many fine houses have dumbwaiters installed, contraptions that draw dishes and heavy objects up and down from the kitchen to dining room. If you inspect the small drawer to your left, you will find a similar contraption involving a small compartment which allows you to send notes to the kitchen, the parlour, and the master bedroom.

This is an ingenious device, popular only here on the Isle of Aster and various countries of the Continent where magic is not the done thing. I know you have been missing the ability to send me a paper bird or other charm to nag me from a short distance, and thus you may enjoy this opportunity.

Mr S.

~

HUSBAND,

You are so thoughtful. I do enjoy nagging you via as many different modes as possible. Are you returned from your walk yet? Bring me tea and cake, if you please, directly to the bedroom.

And take your coat and boots off first!

Mrs S.

WIFE,

You wish me to attend you in the bedroom in my shirt-sleeves? I knew you were a scandalous lady when I married you, but this is beyond the pale.

Mr S.

~

HUSBAND,

I believe you failed to note the most important part of the direction: I want you in your shirtsleeves <u>with tea and cake</u>.

Mrs S.

~

WIFE,

Remove your nightgown and I shall obey.

Mr S.

~

HUSBAND,

What nightgown?

Mrs S.

~

8

FROM: *MRS MNEMOSYNE SEABOURNE, COMFREY COTTAGE, MUDGELY, THE ISLE OF ASTER*

TO: *LADY LIESL OF SANDWICH, STELLAR HOUSE ROYAL APARTMENTS, THE ISLE OF TOWN (REDIRECTED TO APHRODITE VILLA, BRIGHTSIDE, THE ISLE OF BATH)*

MY DEAR FRIEND,

I most certainly shall not answer any of the impertinent questions you put to me in your letter. Why, I am surprised the notepaper did not burst into flames, so saucy your line of inference.

As a married woman, naturally nothing you say can now shock or surprise me, though you are <u>not</u> married and thus should not even know that such questions exist!

Insert several more paragraphs of ladylike tutting...

My husband is most pleasing to me, most generous with his attentions, and our honeymoon has thus far been an exploration of joy and delight. There, I am blushing, and that is all you shall get from me.

Thanks to my husband's new hobby of outdoor walks, there has been a great deal of kissing in hedgerows and canoodling under trees, which caused me a great deal of trepidation at first (you know I am an indoor cat) but has proven rather invigorating.

In other news, have you any advice for removing grass stains from muslin without the use of cleaning charms? We have a day housekeeper, but I cannot bear to show her the state of my things, and I am rapidly running out of outdoor frocks.

Your respectable, blissfully happy friend,
Mrs M. Seabourne

~

WIFE,

We have been invited to visit Bumbleton Palace tomorrow to share a picnic with her Majesty the Queen. Do you wish me to make our excuses? I promised no work for the whole honey-month, and this invitation comes uncomfortably close to a professional engagement.

I should rather spend the day in your company, either way.

Mr S.

~

HUSBAND

Let us not offend her Majesty so soon in our marriage; save it for an anniversary treat. I am sure you would prefer to walk to the Palace, which will mean several hours in my company there and back, with ample opportunity to embrace me on riverbanks which I know is one of your favourite current pastimes.

Therefore, I believe we should accept the royal invitation.

Also, we are out of bread and sardines, I note as a separate matter, if you felt like a wander in the direction of the village.

Your wife (owner of several new bonnets yet to be seen by royalty),

Mrs S.

~

WIFE

I had not considered the many splendid and ample riverbanks between here and Bumbleton Palace, when I suggested we refuse the invitation. You have thoroughly convinced me that we should walk, perhaps with extra time planned in case we are slowed by mud or surprising wildlife.

Mr S.

∾

HUSBAND,

If you think I am meeting the Queen with mud on my hem, you are much mistaken. You shall have to confine your country attentions to less ambitious slopes (or the journey home).

Mrs S.

∾

WIFE,

It is no fault of mine that you look fetching in the sunshine.

Mr S.

∾

HUSBAND,

Perhaps taking a curricle to Bumbleton Palace is to be preferred after all...

Mrs S.

∾

WIFE,

No need for such drastic measures! I shall be on my best behaviour.

Mr S.

~

HUSBAND,

I cannot pay heed to further notes, for I have strayed into a patch of sunshine in the garden, and made myself very comfortable.

Come and find me.

Mrs S.

2

A PICNIC AT BUMBLETON PALACE

"*I*t is not exactly what I imagined," said Mrs
Mnemosyne Seabourne, recently married.

Standing on the hillside overlooking the Queen's
country palace, she considered it with a thoughtful air.
This was a brisk afternoon, for summer. The sun shone,
but as with all corners of this rather small island, there was
a chill sea-breeze that meant it was never wise to walk far
without a shawl.

Luckily, Mneme had several new shawls, thanks to
being drowned in fashionable gifts upon her recent engagement. She should not take it personally, but it did seem as
if her friends had been poised in anticipation of being able
to replace half her wardrobe.

The wedding gift bonanza had also included several
new bonnets, which rather suited her new husband's
newfound devotion to outdoor activities.

Mr C. Thornbury Seabourne, the husband in question,
knew his duty when it came to formal court fashion, and so
today had climbed into waistcoat and breeches instead of

the more comfortable country trousers he had been enjoying on their honeymoon thus far.

He even wore a neatly-tied cravat, having been gifted nearly as many of these fashionable items upon their nuptials as Mneme had received bonnets, shawls and lace-edged smallclothes.

Today's cravat was a splendid grey-blue which matched Thornbury's eyes and made Mneme wish that they were on one of their daily rambles, with no public events to attend.

Duty first. Even on honeymoon, the Queen's wishes must be considered above all things.

"What did you imagine?" said Thornbury. Even as he spoke, his attention was elsewhere, surveying the surrounding hills as if searching for hidden enemies. "Spiralling turrets and peacocks on the lawn?"

"Not necessarily," said Mneme. She rather admired the boxy, modest castle (if a castle could ever be considered modest) and its plain but lush gardens. No peacocks, though from here she could see a sheep or two grazing on the front lawn. She even caught sight of a well-stocked vegetable patch just beyond a tidy hedge of roses.

It was still a palace: a dwelling with so many bedrooms that only a butler could name them all. But it had an oddly cozy, homely feel about it.

"The Royal family like to be comfortable, away from Town," said Thornbury with the casual air of one who had been here before. "I believe her Majesty has a new miraculous gazebo for us to admire."

He had probably visited often throughout his life, given the very specialised work he had undertaken on behalf of his father, the Queen's Consultant (a discreet term for spymaster). Perhaps he was even brought here as a child.

"I like it," Mneme declared. "But are the baths as fine

as those at Wistworia Palace, darling?" She was teasing, though an excuse to call her husband by a pet name was still a delightful novelty.

"Only one way to find out, my dear," replied Thornbury with a twitch of a smile. He offered her his arm, and they walked down the hillside together, towards the country palace.

THE PICNIC TEA was served in a huge summer gazebo garlanded with flowers. So much for modest palace living. Mneme's mother would have been beastly jealous of a gazebo this size, and likely would have ordered one for her own gardens before she even left the party. Thank goodness she wasn't here.

Indeed, the gazebo was the topic of the day, brand-new and, according to the Queen, a gift from a dear friend that had been built over the course of a single miraculous night in a grand feat of extravagant engineering, despite the lack of magic available on the island. With the intricate piecing of the spiny columns and archways that made up the enormous but delicate structure, it seemed impossible that it had not been created by a horde of talented magisters.

There was a mosaic floor and a decorative pool in the centre, with three jewel-bright fish swimming lazily back and forth over bright tiles.

More to the point, Mneme rather felt that once a gazebo was involved, especially one with so many little tables dotted around the place, then one's event could no longer be called a picnic merely because it occurred out-of-doors. Still, she was not the Queen's social secretary, and it was not her call to make.

There were ladies — so many ladies, each in a

sunshine-defying bonnet, which at least added to the picnic air of the event. The permanent residents of Bumbleton Palace were mostly aunties and cousins and relatives so distant that they could never hope to inherit a royal bean but were still somehow eligible for residence in the fanciest bed-and-breakfast of the Teacup Isles.

Mneme was introduced to elderly demi-countesses and marchionesses who had once been Ladies-in-Waiting to the Old Queen, and thus had earned a most sumptuous retirement here, in the middle of nowhere.

There were youngsters, too, clearly dragged along on regular visits in the hopes that Queen Aud — unmarried and childless at nearly twenty-four years of age — would select a favourite urchin to dote upon, and name as her heir.

Only two men were in attendance at this social occasion: Lord Manticore, the Queen's Advisor on Magical Matters, a dour gentleman of dark brows and uncommon tallness whose height was all the more imposing when he folded himself into a lace doily of a chair in a floral gazebo; and Mneme's own husband Mr C. Thornbury Seabourne, who was so immediately set upon by a wave of clucking elderly ladies that she feared she may never see him again.

She ate two bowls of strawberries and cream while waiting for him to emerge from the throng, and began to contemplate a third.

Mneme was not the only outsider here: she found herself standing at the berry table beside Miss Thisbe Wheaten, a very young reporter for *The Gentlewoman*, a popular publication. Miss Wheaten was accompanied by two (even younger) sketch artists, who happily bobbed and weaved around the gazebo, capturing hairstyles and sleeve shapes with a scribble or two of their pencils.

"Are the fashions of the country so interesting to those in town?" asked Mneme, who mostly read *The Gentlewoman* for the embroidery patterns and, on occasion, the reviews of popular novels.

"Why, yes," gasped Miss Wheaten, piling her plate high with cakes. "Her Majesty is so generous — very generous indeed. Always turns out in something new, to create a fashionable mode when all else is quiet. It's really most delightful of her."

As if to prove her point, Queen Aud made her appearance at that moment, accompanied by one rather sour-looking lady-in-waiting. The two of them were garbed as shepherdesses, or rather in the manner of wealthy ladies playing at shepherdesses. They wore fluffy bonnets and flouncing gowns covered in flowers, with daisy bracelets. Both of them carried shepherd crooks covered in silk ribbons.

The Queen's warm brown skin tones and curly black hair looked marvellous in the dainty china-doll fashions, while her pale, blonde and less amicable lady-in-waiting looked very much as if she had been costumed against her will.

"Majestic!" squealed Miss Wheaten. "Inspired!" She darted forward to ask the Queen a few questions about her new fashion statement.

Their monarch was clever, Mneme realised, watching how her Majesty stopped to answer Miss Wheaten's questions, rather than making a beeline for the sandwiches and higher ranked guests. The kind of publicity she would gain from the effusively grateful young reporter would come across as entirely genuine and lacking in artifice. *The Gentlewoman* was found in every drawing room and dressmaker's establishment; no man would have thought of the propaganda value of such a publication.

17

"Within a week, all the young ladies of Town will be wearing their own lace bonnets and ordering shepherd's crooks bedecked with ribbons," said Thornbury, appearing at his wife's side with a plate of sandwiches and a spare cup of tea, like the magician he was. "I don't think her Majesty is ever given nearly enough credit for her sense of humour."

"I'm sure the ribbon shops will be praising her name," said Mneme, accepting the cup with a happy sigh. "Who's that lady with her? The other shepherdess. The one who looks like she's eaten a lemon."

"Mrs Cheshire," said Thornbury, in a tone she rarely heard from him; wariness verging on dislike. "Her official title is social secretary. But she hasn't been seen in Town for years; some sort of unofficial exile."

"Gossiping, husband?"

"Never, wife!" He piled a few cucumber sandwiches on the edge of Mneme's saucer. "Eat up. You must build your strength for the walk home."

"Home." She smiled at him. "I like the sound of that."

They would have a true home of their own, soon enough. Mneme's cousin Henry was having a house renovated for the happy couple on the Isle of Storm, on the other side of the village from his own country residence Storm North. He insisted it was the least he could do as a wedding gift for his dear friend and his cousin. Mneme and Thornbury were well aware his generosity had a lot to do with wanting them conveniently close at hand, as Henry relied so much on Thornbury's advice and expertise. It was an arrangement they had accepted with reluctant grace, but the renovations of Tempest Manse had now been carrying on for longer than expected. At this rate, they would have to extend their honeymoon. Such trials!

"You survived the mob, at least," Mneme noted,

turning her attention to the gazebo full of aunties, many of whom were still making eyes at her husband. "Isn't it odd to have so many noblewomen in one place, and not a single one trying to cast a spell on another?"

No hint of magic about the tea things, either, no preservation spells to keep teapots hot or cream cakes cool. It was an altogether unusual scene to Mneme, who had lived her entire live immersed in background magic. Even after a week here on this island, she kept being surprised by it all.

"You say odd, I say relaxing," remarked Thornbury. "Barely a hint of magical resonance in the air, and no one trying to kidnap anyone. I can't believe I never thought of holidaying on the Isle of Aster before." He gave the gazebo a meaningful look, as if it was a mystery he needed to solve at some point.

"Well," said Mneme, giving him an impish smile. "Perhaps you did not have the right incentive before."

He widened his eyes at her in warm mockery. "I can't think what you mean, Mrs Seabourne."

They enjoyed the picnic thoroughly; their first official social outing as a married couple. Like children playing house together, they delighted in beating each other to introductions as they circulated the gazebo.

"Have you met my wife, Mrs Seabourne?"

"Do let me introduce you to my husband, Mr Seabourne."

Quite sickening, as Mneme's dear friend Juno might remark, if she were here.

The Seabournes managed a full hour of social niceties and teasing each other before Lord Manticore interrupted, introducing them both to his wife Lady Persimmon before immediately drawing Thornbury away for 'a moment of your time.'

Thornbury hesitated, conscious of work intruding on their holiday, but Mneme had promised him ahead of time she would not be petty about such things. They knew that a Palace visit would come at a cost sooner or later. Now, she simply smiled and allowed him to disappear from the gazebo without complaint.

Lady Persimmon Manticore was beautiful. She had long, dark hair wrapped up in braids beneath her saffron bonnet, which Mneme instantly envied. It was a colour she herself could never wear thanks to her red hair. Lady Persimmon's gown was up-to-the-minute fashionable, as well, all bold colouring and generous neckline.

Mneme had never met Lady Persimmon before; she was one of those wives who remained in the country while her husband was occupied in Town and Court on the Queen's business. There were two kinds of married ladies in aristocratic society: those who took command of the social whirl, and those who disappeared into the domesticity of private estates, at least until their children were old enough to be sent away to school. Perhaps that would change now that ladies had the freedom of portal travel.

Mneme was certainly the last person to judge another for wanting to avoid social occasions as much as possible.

"I suppose we should be honoured," Lady Persimmon said dryly. "The gentlemen stayed in our company for a full tea service before making their excuses to escape."

Mneme was a little offended at the idea that her husband might be actively trying to avoid her, but she kept it to herself. The second round of tea was indeed being served now, fresh pots carried from the kitchens, and she made sure to hold her own cup out for a footman to refill. It was vital not to hesitate, when natural heating methods were the only way to keep the tea at the proper temperature.

"You're one of those Seabournes, aren't you?" asked Lady Manticore.

"I suppose I am," said Mneme, remaining polite. Given the recent scandals and dramas in her family, a little passive aggression was to be expected. "Do you visit the Isle of Aster very often?"

Lady Persimmon stiffened slightly, as if Mneme had made some accusation. "It is convenient, of course, to our own country seat," she said, sipping her own tea. "Just across the bridge from the Isle of Manticore. And the children do so enjoy the lake. We own a small holiday villa on the shore, where we like to stay when the Queen is in residence, so the children have a chance of seeing their father. Besides, they love the fresh air and the mud."

"It is a very pretty lake," Mneme agreed. "Mr Seabourne and I have enjoyed many local walks while staying in Mudgely."

A server placed a tray of sweet biscuits and cakes on a nearby table, which was immediately swarmed by a small horde of rapscallions: two nut-brown children, one pale with a shock of blond curls, all rather mud-splashed and trailing un-tied boots and waistcoats from what must once have been very nice outfits.

"Freddie, Alfie, Ed," said Lady Persimmon sharply. "Mind your manners."

The boys apologised quickly, shuffled their feet, and then made off for the nearest bush with their pockets full of cream cakes.

Mneme found herself smiling: she had never been especially fond of children, but something about being newly married made her feel softer and more tolerant of scamps with sticky fingers. "Yours?" she inquired.

Again, there was that slightly defensive twitch, as if something impolite had been implied.

"Two of them," Lady Persimmon said quickly. "And another at home in the nursery."

"Lovely," Mneme murmured.

It was so very awkward, to be caught in conversation with someone one did not know, who quite clearly wished to be elsewhere. Luckily for them both, the Queen provided a well-timed interruption.

"My dear guests!" she cried, standing on a chair with extreme gumption, aided by the deferential (but still stony-faced) Lord Manticore, now back at her side. "What a lovely picnic, thank you so much for joining us. I am so very pleased to announce that next week, we shall be celebrating my dear Lord Manticore's name day here at the palace with a Midsummer Masque! I do hope you will all attend. Please give your names to Mrs Cheshire if you wish an invitation. I want simply everyone to come!"

Mneme had only been paying half-attention to the Queen's announcement, except to note that the shepherdess costume only added to their monarch's excessively giddy manner. Perhaps she had consumed too many sugary cakes.

She glanced around for her husband, realising that Lord Manticore's presence at the Queen's side meant that Thornbury must surely no longer be engaged.

Quite by accident, she caught an expression of embarrassment on the face of Lady Persimmon Manticore, this time directed at her husband, still steadying the Queen with one cautious hand as she stepped down from her chair.

Oh, Mneme realised in one horrible moment as she saw the Queen tip her face up with a glowing smile for her Advisor on Magical Matters, and he replied with a look of fond impatience. *They're in love with each other. And his wife knows.*

3

AN UNEXPECTED TOUR OF
UNSETTLING ARTEFACTS

"*M*ay I help you, Mrs Seabourne?"

After the third round of tea came and went, with no sighting of Mr C. Thornbury Seabourne, Mneme took it upon herself to go hunting for her husband. Thanks to the useful advice of several maids and a royal great aunt (something removed), she found herself here: in a bright hallway somewhere on the ground floor of Bumbleton Palace, at an enormous door covered in bronze carvings of lions. A closed door, guarded by a sour-faced woman with golden curls and the unwelcome costume of a china shepherdess: Mrs Cheshire, the Queen's social secretary.

Mneme put on the brightest smile that she often used when she wanted a person to underestimate her. "Why, hello. You must be Mrs Cheshire. I'm looking for my husband. Have you seen him?"

Mrs Cheshire smiled in return: a thoroughly unfriendly expression that felt closer to mockery than politeness. "I'm afraid Mr Seabourne is in a meeting right now, and cannot be disturbed."

Mneme considered this information. "Not with Lord Manticore," she said, for she had of course seen him return to the party.

"No, Mrs Seabourne," said Mrs Cheshire. "Not with Lord Manticore." She offered no further information.

Mneme narrowed her eyes slightly. "And may I ask —" Clearly, she may not.

"Have you seen the Moonlight Gallery?" Mrs Cheshire said abruptly, and with surprising enthusiasm.

"Excuse me?" Mneme said, not quite sure why this unpleasant person was suddenly radiating friendliness. "I'm afraid I don't quite —"

"Do let me show you you."

To Mneme's complete surprise, Mrs Cheshire tucked their arms together as if they were the greatest of friends, and marched her up the length of the hallway. They spiralled up a gleaming white staircase, and hurried along a terraced corridor until they arrived at what appeared to be a terrifying museum of theatrical antiquities, in a room with more curtains than seemed remotely practical.

The curtains began at a high peak on one side of the room — presumably the outer wall of the castle. They were thick and heavy velvet, deep red with gold tassels. They fell in layers, with looping cords. If there were really windows enough to justify quite so much curtainage, then someone must have bought out a glass factory to build them all.

The exhibits were mostly masks, both the elegant kind with beading and ribbons that one saw at river festivals, and also the whole-head variety that were generally used to frighten children in parades and pantomimes. They filled the room, hanging on wires and mounted on velvet-draped plinths. Where there were not curtains, there were shelves on which more masks and props and patchwork garments were arranged. Mneme might have found them beautiful and interesting as individual pieces, but crammed together in this display of grandiose excess, they radiated a distinct sense of threat.

"Goodness," she said, for something to say. "What a collection."

"Isn't it simply phantasmagoric?" said Mrs Cheshire, acting for all the world as if her only intentions here were friendship, with a hint of education. "The Queen's great-grandfather, King Osbert, adored masks and costumes. Apparently he used to chase maids around the Palace while disguised as a donkey." She indicated an enormous donkey head mask, suspended from the ceiling. It looked like it was constructed from the corpse of a quite unhealthy example of the breed. It had been painted white at one point, and covered in spangles, but the texture was undeniably that of genuine donkey hide.

"How very…" Mneme was not going to say charming. "Historical. And what a lot of curtains." Curtains, surely, made for a safe topic.

"That's why this is called the Moonlight Gallery," said Mrs Cheshire. "King Osbert was mad about moonlight. He had this room designed so he could look upon his trea-sures by the light of a full moon. Of course, we can't have the curtains open during the day, or everything would fade."

"Of course," Mneme echoed. "Mrs Cheshire, is there something you want to tell me?" It was not the first time that someone had drawn her aside at a social occasion and said something mysterious in the hopes she would pass the message on to Thornbury. People had been doing it from the moment they announced their engagement. A select few members of society knew that he had worked as a secret agent for the Crown, and hardly anyone knew of his connexion to the Queen's spymaster, Octavian Swift (after all, almost nobody knew Mr Swift's true role in Her Majesty's government). But as Mneme had learned once she herself was brought in on the secret, nearly everyone who was *anyone* knew that Thornbury worked for the Duke of Storm, and that if sinister mysteries were brought to the attention of either of those two men, they would be sorted out swiftly.

Mrs Cheshire was playing it completely straight: no winking or careful emphasis on words as she perambulated around the room in her pink and white shepherdess gown. Perhaps the woman really did just want to show Mneme a palace curiosity to keep her busy while…

Ah, while Thornbury had his mysterious appointment. Got it. This wasn't an attempt to pass a message, it was an attempt to keep Mneme away from her husband's secret business.

"We should really return to the gazebo," Mneme said gently, unhooking her arm from Mrs Cheshire's. "I would not wish to offend the Queen."

"Indeed not," a familiar voice rang across the gallery of masks, costumes and curtains.

Mneme glanced up and felt a warm smile overtake her whole body as she spied her husband standing there in the doorway. "Hello, dear."

"Mrs Seabourne," Thornbury said in a tone she had started to recognise as teasing. "It's not like you to wander off."

"I know, darling, but I really *had* to have a conversation about palace curtains with Mrs Cheshire."

It was as if he only now realised they were not alone in the room: Thornbury's eyes went to Mrs Cheshire and froze there for a moment.

26

"How nice to see you, Thornbury," she said in a pleasant tone.

Mneme rankled at the familiarity; of course, his old acquaintances would be used to calling him by the surname he had now taken as his given name. In this case, it presumed a familiarity that left Mneme quite unsettled, not because Mrs Cheshire was a beautiful woman (which of course, she was) but because she spoke to him as might a colleague and an equal. Thornbury's colleagues were not, on the whole, the nicest or safest of people to be around.

"And you, Electra," he replied with a nod, then immediately pretended she was no longer present, all his attention locked on Mneme. "Shall we go down, my dear? There's a round of ices to come, before the Queen sends us all packing to work on our masquerade costumes. All the best royal occasions come with homework, after all."

"Oh, ices!" said Mneme, knowing a change of subject when she heard one. "I do hope they have artichoke, it's my favourite."

"You should take the back stairs," Mrs Cheshire called after them.

"Nonsense," said Thornbury, taking Mneme's arm firmly in his and whisking her off down the corridor, away from the spangled carnival masks, and grotesque stuffed animal heads.

"A secret meeting," she said in a low voice. "Today?"

"Couldn't be helped," he said lightly. "Do you think they're still serving tea? I'm parched."

"It won't be hot," she warned.

"I suppose I deserve that."

On the ground floor of Bumbleton Palace, as Thornbury steered them speedily along, they crossed in front of the enormous door covered in bronze lion carvings. The door was ajar and just for a moment, Mneme thought she caught sight of a sleeve, and the side of someone's head, before the door firmly shut again.

Still, it was enough. She wouldn't forget that particular profile in a hurry. Octavian Swift, her father-in-law. He had not attended the wedding, nor had he sent a gift.

But apparently he did not hesitate to summon her (retired!) husband into secret palace meetings while they were on their honeymoon.

"I won't ask what all that was about," Mneme said, as they returned to the Queen's picnic in the impossible gazebo.

"Thank you," replied her husband. "It's a minor matter, I promise. Nothing to worry about."

He had chosen the front stairs; had given her an opportunity to see a glimpse of what he was dealing with. Good. That was the kind of husband he intended to be.

Thornbury had already learned a lesson that his father had yet to absorb: it was never wise to get on the wrong side of a Seabourne.

4

TEA PARTIES FOR THE MAGICALLY
INCLINED

For as long as there had been magic in the
Teacup Isles, there had been Seabourne
women. Mnemosyne came from a long line of wives,
mothers and daughters with red-gold hair, a talent for
meddling, and an extraordinary wealth of magical power.

It was said that their ancestress Selene Seabourne was
on the original ship that discovered the Teacup Isles,
centuries past, and was the first to realise how much magic
was stored here: in the air, in the land, in every blade of
grass.

(This was, it had to be said, a highly edited version of
the history of the early Seabournes, which failed to
acknowledge how many of the family's greatest sorceresses
had not always been the nicest or most socially responsible
of people.)

Still, *magic*. It was important to her family, more than
social reputation (which was currently dented thanks to the
behaviour of a rogue aunt) or rank (something Mneme had
used to her advantage when choosing a professional

husband whom some narrow-minded folk might consider to be below her station).

And so, on the day after the Queen's tea party, when Mneme awoke alone to find a letter from Thornbury excusing him from her company for the morning, she decided to set out in search of what little magic the Isle of Aster had to offer.

She didn't *require* magic. But she was somewhat homesick for the ability to light a candle without hunting for a tinderbox.

According to rumour, provided by Mrs Standish in the Mudgely village shop, as well as several of the Queen's aunties, there was the occasional secret pocket of magic to be found around Aster, if you looked for it carefully and did not mind the risk of getting your feet wet.

The lake path was indeed rather damp, and even soggy in places, but Mneme had thought ahead and chosen her old walking boots, the ones that would never recover their original shine but remained comfortable and laden with robust waterproofing charms. Magic might not be able to be cast here on the Isle of Aster, but the effects of magic held up against its fresh air; it would take more than the month Mneme was staying here for those particular charms to wear away.

The instruction was to look for the place where the buttercups turned blue, but she had been walking for half an hour past the village, and was yet to spot any buttercups at all.

Just as she was reaching the stage of feeling extremely foolish, she was greeted by the owner of a ruffled parasol and some extremely fashionable boots with pearl buttons on glossy rose-pink leather.

"Hello, there!"

Mneme tipped back her own parasol and smiled politely. "Good morning."

The ruffled parasol shifted, and a young lady emerged from beneath it, dressed in the recently-launched fashion of a china shepherdess, all flounces and ribbons. There was a swirl of chestnut hair, pinned up in an attempt at a matronly arrangement beneath a fluffy hat, but the overall impression was that someone had attempted to out-ruffle the Queen in shades of pale pink and green.

"Are you looking for blue buttercups?" said the ruffled lady with a dazzling smile. "You have that look about you."

"Is it so obvious?"

"Come on, I'll show you!" Like a poodle hunting a rat, the young lady drew Mneme away from the lake path and up the slope, her gown bobbing as she went. "I'm simply famished, aren't you?"

Mneme blinked, unsure if she was expected to eat the bluebells. "I wasn't really…"

Then she saw it. A tiny thatched cottage, with a brightly colourful floral bed out the front, so pretty that it might have been peeled from a children's book about hedgehogs in mobcaps and aprons. Still no buttercups in sight.

As they drew close, what looked like a plain white cloth blowing in the summer breeze resolved itself into a sign with the painted letters spelling out the words: The Blue Buttercup, Cake and Teas.

"I do like that cake comes before teas," said her new companion with a happy sigh. "It shows the correct priorities." She gave Mneme a firm look. "You *were* hunting for magic, weren't you?"

Indeed, she was, and she had found it. Mneme inhaled the air, enjoying that pleasing pulse which meant her magic was awake again, and ready to be fed. Much though she had enjoyed the refreshing novelty of her magic-free honeymoon house — *this* felt like home.

"But a tea shop?" Mneme said, still wrapping her head around it all.

Her new companion trilled with laughter. "Oh, well. If you found a magical pocket lying around on an unmagical island, wouldn't you start your own tea shop right on that very spot? In the old days, we'd have been huddled around a buttercup patch, muttering spells at each other in secret. Now at least we can order refreshments and sit upon straight-backed chairs. So very civilised, don't you know?"

The young matron ushered Mneme into the cottage, and a loud bell clanged to herald their arrival. "I'm Mrs Phoebe Holiday," she said with the confidence of a person who had already decided they were going to be friends. "Charmed to make your acquaintance."

"Mrs Mnemosyne Seabourne," said Mneme, giving in to the inevitable. "Charmed to make yours." She had come looking for magic and now, apparently, she was to socialise and make friends. Why was this always happening to her?

Phoebe clapped her hands in delight, since apparently she was the sort of person who did that sort of thing without a trace of irony. "Splendid! Let's have a mountain of scones."

MNEME DID NOT CONSIDER herself a snob, and yet there was nothing like a cup of tea properly heated and kept at the correct temperature by magic. She inhaled two of them, while learning various 'new acquaintance facts' about Mrs Phoebe Holiday, who had moved to Mudgely six months earlier, with a husband about whom she revealed little.

Her chatter suggested she was starved for company, and yet she clearly had no trouble making local friends; she was at the Blue Buttercup today to meet with a small party, though they had not yet arrived.

Used to being around ladies who talked more than she did, Mneme was happy to drink her tea in the warm surroundings of familiar magic, while letting the conversation wash over her. She contributed a little, when there was a pause, though Phoebe did not seem to mind doing most of the work.

It was a surprise, then, when the door to the cottage tea room clanged open again, and one of Phoebe's friends finally arrived: the rather solemn Lady Persimmon Manticore.

"Persie!" Phoebe cried out, embracing her friend and hustling her to the table. "Do come and meet Mneme. Wait, I must do the rounds of your imps."

A nursemaid with a large perambulator had followed Lady Persimmon into the tea room, along with the children Mneme remembered from the garden party. The boys, the baby and their nursemaid all arranged themselves at a separate table, ordering tea and sandwiches. The boys happily immersed themselves in a popular game involving small marbles of coloured light, which of course could only be played in a magical space.

Phoebe did her dutiful rounds, kissing and/or clucking at each of the children, politely asking the nursemaid about the health of her mother, and then returned to the table in time to bully Lady Persimmon into ordering a much larger selection of cake than she had originally intended.

"No sign of Electra?" she asked carelessly as the waitress took their order. "Goodness, I suppose she's busy these days."

Mneme blinked in surprise. She had not expected Mrs Cheshire to be one of Phoebe's circle, and rather dreaded the possibility of having to be friendly with her over cakes.

"She'll be along sooner or later," said Lady Persimmon, with a meaningful glance towards the boys. She took in Mrs Holiday's extraordinary outfit. "Really, Phoebe?"

"Now, dearest, what is the point of having friends above my station if I can't learn about the newest fashions before they hit the ladies' magazines?" said Phoebe with a shameless grin.

Lady Persimmon shook her head, barely concealing a smile. "And how do you do, Mrs Seabourne? Are you enjoying your stay on the Isle of Aster?"

"Very much," said Mneme, pleased that Lady Persimmon seemed more inclined towards friendly conversation than she had at their previous meeting. The presence of Phoebe was likely responsible; it was impossible to be grumpy in proximity to such a pure ray of sunshine.

The three ladies drank several rounds of tea with scones, floating lemon-thyme wafers, and strawberry madeleines.

Phoebe led the gossip, with new topics introduced every time a fresh cake hit the table. It was one of the best teas that Mneme had ever attended. Finally, as the conversation reached a rare lull, she was able to ask about the Blue Buttercup itself.

"Is this the only magical spot on the island?"

"Goodness no," said Phoebe. "I know of at least five. Persie?"

"Nine," said Lady Persimmon, cracking a wafer between her teeth. One of her small boys ran over to show her a drawing and she nodded, smiled, and sent him back with a few bright pink cakes to share with the others at the nursery table. "Not all of them are quite as hospitable as this, though. And there's a tenth famously that no one has ever been able to locate because it moves from place to place."

"There's a tiny one in the park on the far side of the lake," said Phoebe. "Not large enough for even the smallest of tea rooms, tragically. Though I believe some smart fellow popped a postbox upon it, to enchant letters home."

"There's one up on the moors beyond the salmon tarns," Lady Persimmon volunteered. "But I don't recommend going up there alone. Not with —" She gave Phoebe a quick look, then fell silent.

"Never mind all bunk about mysterious monsters roaming the moors," said Phoebe, dismissing it with a wave of her hand. "Betty Winthrop from the stationer's in the village said that the Queen's invitations went out this morning. What are we all going to wear to the Midsummer Masque?"

"I hadn't thought about it," said Mneme quickly. She found all forms of costume party deeply embarrassing, and had put the whole event out of her mind.

"I won't get to choose for myself," said Lady Persimmon with a wry twist of her mouth. "The costume will arrive as a royal command. But at least I know whatever I wear won't offend the Queen…"

Mneme had not even thought about the possibility of offending Her Majesty with her masquerade costume. This was why she liked to steer clear of such affairs!

"Ah, how tiresome it is to be a court favourite," said Phoebe teasingly. "Whereas I'm lucky to be on the invitation list at all, as the wife of a—"

"Local dignitary?" said Lady Persimmon, also teasing.

"Eh, as if the Queen hand-selects your costume," said Phoebe. "Surely that's Mrs Cheshire's job?"

"Depends how high you are on the list of favourites," replied Lady Persimmon. For some reason, what Phoebe had said embarrassed her a little; she avoided eye contact for a moment, concentrating on her teacup

"I heard that the Countess of Sandwich was going to come dressed as an actual sandwich," Phoebe went on. "Such a strange lady, from all reports. Second wife, of course…"

"I'm sure Mrs Seabourne doesn't wish to hear frivolous gossip," said Lady Persimmon, rolling her eyes.

"Oh, I love frivolous gossip," Mneme insisted. "I'm a fiend for it, ask anyone. Gossip away!"

She thought she saw a twitch of a smile on Lady Persimmon's lips, and considered that a victory.

THEIR TEA PARTY came to an end without any further mention of the guest that was supposed to join them. Mrs Electra Cheshire was clearly off selecting flattering (or unflattering) masquerade costumes for the Queen's favourites, and had no time for rosewater squares or honey jumbles.

To Mneme's surprise, Lady Persimmon packed her children and nursemaid off in the direction of their holiday villa, along the lake path, giving the scamps kisses for being good in the tea room. She then turned back to the ladies with determination. "We will walk you home, Mrs Seabourne."

"We will?" said Phoebe in surprise. "I mean, of course we will!"

"Safety in numbers," said Lady Persimmon primly.

"We shall walk Mrs Seaborne home, and then you may walk me home."

Mneme wanted to ask why they were so conscious of safety in a tiny village like this — surely not because of the so-called beast on the moors? She stayed quiet though, certain she would learn more from silence than from questions.

"And I shall stay with you forever," said Phoebe, still focused upon teasing Lady P.

Lady Persimmon rolled her eyes and offered another of those secret smiles. Clearly, she liked Phoebe's company rather more than she preferred to admit. "You may stay with me until your husband comes to collect you."

"Oh, I suppose so," said Phoebe with a cheerful sigh. "Persie and I are plagued by working husbands, Mneme. I suppose you are in the same boat."

"I knew it when I married him," Mneme agreed, only a little ruefully.

"I thought mine was terribly neglectful until I made friends with Persie," Phoebe confessed. "But hers is hardly home at all! I suppose one can't argue with Queen and Country, but it must be such a terrible bore."

"I get by," said Lady Persimmon, with no sign of a smile this time.

They had only walked a little way up the path towards the village when Mneme caught sight of something that gave her pause: a lady's boot, small and buttoned, splayed across the edge of the path. A step close and she could see a stockinged ankle connected to that boot.

The other ladies saw it in the same instant. Phoebe's careless chatter fell suddenly silent.

Lady Persimmon looked as if she had been struck. "No," she murmured, then threw herself forward. "*Electra!*"

Somehow Mneme already knew to hold on to her, pull her back from the cluster of bushes beside the path... but it was not fast enough to prevent her from seeing... to prevent any of them from seeing the fallen, lifeless body of Mrs Cheshire, social secretary to the Queen.

This had been no accident. Mrs Cheshire looked surprised, even in death, and there were marks on her neck: silvery vein patterns that Mneme recognised from her own long history with spells and sorcery.

The Queen's social secretary had been murdered with magic, on an island where that should be entirely impossible.

Lady Persimmon, once she realised that the other woman was truly dead, began to scream.

5

YOU ARE CORDIALLY INVITED TO A
MURDER SCENE

*M*neme liked to think of herself as the sort of person who was good in a crisis, but it was the bubbly Phoebe Holiday who took charge the moment that they found the unexpected body on the village path.

It was Phoebe who checked that Mrs Cheshire was indeed dead, and Phoebe who darted back to the tea room in order to use their localised magic to call for help, while Mneme stayed with the inconsolable Lady Persimmon.

This unexpected practical streak in Phoebe finally made sense once the local constabulary — including a very gruff police inspector — arrived on the scene to take care of matters.

Phoebe hurled herself into the inspector's arms and burst into tears. It was only then that Mneme realised, belatedly, what her new friend's over-worked husband did for a living.

She was in shock, she decided later. Not so much because of the presence of a dead body, which was not entirely a new experience. But it had been such a lovely day, and now something awful had happened to a woman

39

she did not like, but who was clearly loved by Lady Persimmon and Phoebe. If they were so fond of the deceased woman, there must have been something more to her than a sharp tongue.

Later, as she was being escorted home by police carriage, it also occurred to Mneme that they might not be the only people who would mourn Mrs Cheshire. The Queen, of course, would be distraught. Thornbury… he had a history with the woman, too. She had been a colleague of his, in the past. And if Mrs Cheshire had crossed professional paths with Thornbury, that suggested she had also worked with his sinister and intimidating father, Octavian Swift.

~

COMFREY COTTAGE WAS EMPTY. Their housekeeper had been and gone for the day, leaving the front parlour spick and span as usual (and probably leaving some kind of delicious pie in the larder for their supper, the woman was a gem).

Mneme did not get as far as the parlour, because there was a donkey head in the entry hall.

Indeed, there was an entire packing crate someone had left there, with a palace seal on one side of it. And, resting on top of the packing crate: the head of a donkey.

It was not, to be clear, a realistic head. Nor was it the horrifying clearly-made-from-a-real-animal monstrosity she had seen at the Palace, as part of that bewildering display of royal masks. This donkey head was also white and gold, but made from papier-mâché and studded with paste jewels. Its eyes glowed an unholy green colour, and the mane was constructed from slashed silk ribbons.

It was a mask. Of course it was a mask. Still, its overall

appearance was deeply unsettling, particularly as she had just come from a scene of unexpected death. Mneme reached out for the gold envelope jammed beneath the donkey head, and levered it open carefully, reading the card inside.

❧

You are cordially invited
To Bumbleton Palace
To celebrate a Midsummer Masque
In honour of the name day of
ALFRED, LORD MANTICORE,
Favourite minister of the Queen

❧

THERE WERE a few more details in flowery lettering, including what was clearly a stern reminder of what an honour it was to have one's costume personally selected by her Majesty. There, in the far corner of the elaborately printed card, was a signature. *Electra Cheshire.*

"Darling."

It was Thornbury, letting himself in through the front door. He looked entirely rumpled, and quite concerned. Dressed formally, Mneme noted, so he had been working today and not merely off on a ramble.

He came to her immediately, checking her over to ensure she was unharmed before he allowed himself to embrace her. "Are you well?"

"You've heard," Mneme said numbly. She had girded herself to be the one to tell him of Mrs Cheshire's unexpected death.

"News travels fast on a small island." He did not elaborate on where, or with whom, he had been today, but turned his face into her hair for a moment, then kissed the side of her neck. "You smell like magic."

"I found a secret tea room."

"Of course you did. You're not hurt?"

"Whoever killed her was long gone when we found her." Shivering, she described to him the patterns she had seen on Mrs Cheshire's neck and face.

Thornbury nodded grimly. "Magic where it should not be," he said. "Was she far from the Blue Buttercup?"

That was an interesting thought. One could of course cast small magics on another person at a distance — sympathetic magic from a wax dolly or a poppet using the subject's hair or nail clipping. A knotted thread, a point on a map. Subjects could be nudged, or lured, or even enchanted.

But a curse powerful enough to kill? That could not be done without a source of magic immediately to hand, and the victim within line of site.

"Too far," said Mneme, shaking her head, certain of it. "And too many trees and shrubs. The path was sheltered. Perhaps if someone stood on a boat, they might have been able to see her…"

"No magical pockets on the lake," Thornbury said, as if this was a known fact.

"Isn't there one that moves?" she asked, remembering that detail from her conversation with Phoebe and Persimmon.

Thornbury's face closed over. "There is indeed," he said warily. "But if that one is involved, her murderer did not work at a distance."

❦

AFTER THEY HAD CALMED themselves with a restorative cup of tea (Thornbury's ability to produce one from an unstaffed kitchen was one of the many delightful surprises about their marriage thus far; clearly he had spent many years living in bachelor rooms before he was stolen and spoiled by the Duke of Storm's employ), Mneme and Thornbury repaired to the parlour so that she could explain every detail of her day to him.

The island's gossip mills had indeed been active, as nothing she had to say was surprising to him — even that her new friend was married to the local police inspector!

"Gordon Holiday," he said, with an approving nod. "Sensible fellow. He's asked me to consult with them on the magical nature of Mrs Cheshire's death." He gave Mneme a swift look, clearly seeing the concern in her eyes. "I know I promised work would not interfere with our honeymoon."

"It's not that," she said quickly. "Obviously, one can't help a murder on our doorstep. But, Thornbury. Are you sure it would be wise to be involved? You knew her personally."

An odd look crossed his face. "All the more reason to see that justice is done in the matter of her murder."

Mneme nodded slowly. "I understand." She also had many more questions, but wasn't quite ready to voice them yet. "My dear, may I ask —" He tensed at that, clearly not ready for the questions this case might provoke for them both. As it happened, her question was closer to home than he might expect. "What exactly is the situation with the decapitated ass in the hallway?"

Thornbury gave a short laugh, his eyes sad. "That, my dear, would appear to be a final insult from a complicated woman."

"And you're planning to wear it, to the Masque?"

"I don't believe I have any choice, not if the Queen has decreed it. Even by proxy." He patted Mneme's hair. "Don't worry. I'm sure your costume is far more flattering than mine."

"That wasn't quite what I was worrying about," Mneme said tartly. Even in death, somehow, Mrs Cheshire was managing to have a dig at them both.

6

TACTFUL CORRESPONDENCE OF A
DISCREET NATURE

FROM: *THE DUCHESS OF STORM, STORM BOLT,
THE ISLE OF TOWN*

TO: *THE NEW MRS MNEMOSYNE SEABOURNE,
COMFREY COTTAGE, MUDGELY, THE ISLE OF
ASTER*

*D*arling Mnemosyne,
     Of course we shall attend the Midsummer
Masque. You know Henry can never say no to a party. And
thanks to the blissful portal revolution (aren't you clever!)
we need never turn down an invitation again.

     (Thank you for your inquiry as to my health. I am
mostly quite content though occasionally require a sudden
tray of ginger tea and dry biscuits to get me through the
later part of the afternoon; my maids are trained to fetch it
the moment they spot a trace of green upon my
complexion.)

I have purchased a magnificent costume for the occasion, while my husband threatens to come disguised as either a lion or a unicorn. You will forgive me if I trip and fall and 'accidentally' go home with an entirely different husband out of sheer embarrassment...

(Not your husband, of course, my dear, I have some discretion!)

Speaking of discretion, I was fascinated to hear you inquire about the mysterious Mrs C, who met such an unfortunate end in recent days. What a to-do! Of course I know of her, though even with my correspondence triple-hexed to prevent it from being read by any eyes by yours, I am not sure how much would be appropriate to record on the page.

You know of course that Henry went to Delphi College for a year or so, for larks, before he remembered that as a peer of the realm he had no need to bother with formal qualifications? I believe it was some kind of punishment detail devised by his mother, or aunts, after he transformed a flower bed into some kind of rampaging lightning monster (in fact, I believe the creature still resides on the far side of the Isle of Storm, in some kind of domestic arrangement with several ogres).

WELL, that's where they met, of course. H and your new Mr S, and the lovely Electra Melusine as she was, one of the Sandwich Melusines, and that Cheshire fellow she later married. Edmund. Edfried? Edwardius. He was a curse crafter, you know, devised simply devilish spells, the kind that are terribly complicated and then everyone forgets they haven't been there forever. I believe he came up with Toasting Stones. And Diamond Hexes! And those little bells you can hang on your cat's collar in order to spy through their eyes.

Anyway, Edwinium blew himself up doing something

or other, spell design gone horribly wrong. I think they have a child, tucked away somewhere? By then, Mrs C was thoroughly established as one of the Queen's favourites, she ran simply all the parties in Town, and you did not want to get on the wrong side of her let me tell you.

I'm terribly embarrassed, though, I can't remember at all what the scandal was that got her sent down to Bumbleton, I know it was hushed up at the time but that usually means that simply everyone knows the gory details! What a failure I am as a friend. I have a feeling it might have all happened when I was in mourning for Mr Von Trask (my Husband #1, wretched hunting accident), or possibly it was the year that the Season was cancelled due to mouse plague and we were all writing novels to each other to pass the time? I'll ask around for you, tactfully, of course. Discretion is my middle name.

Much love,

Juno, Duchess of Discretion

~

FROM: *THE DUKE OF STORM, STORM BOLT, THE ISLE OF TOWN*

TO: *THE NEW MRS MNEMOSYNE SEABOURNE, COMFREY COTTAGE, MUDGELY, THE ISLE OF ASTER*

What Ho, Mnemo!

Hope you and Thornbury are having a topping time on the Isle of Aster. Can't stand the place, myself, what's the point of having magic and not being able to use it to light your cigars or recolour your cravats at a moment's notice?

I've instructed Bellings to box up those books you asked for, about magical assassinations and the history of magic-free islands and all that other what-not.

Surprised old Thornbury didn't ask me himself, you know I'm always happy to help! It's been rather dull here over the last few weeks, what with the Matter of The Ginger Tea. Juno has quite taken against any social engagements outside the house, though we'll be frocking up for the Midsummer Masque next week, don't you worry about that!

(Not that I'm complaining, don't tell her I'm complaining, she thew a vase at my head last week when I said, rather jovially I thought, that these were the sacrifices we make for heirs, don't you know.)

I rather fancy dressing up as a unicorn. Especially if Thorners is going to be a donkey. Ha! That reminds me of a funny story from our college years (a year and a half in my case, really, before I was sent down) that I am certainly not going to tell you even if I've been at the port-wine. Got to preserve some of one's chums' secrets for when we're old and grey.

Anyhoo, hit me up for more deposits from the Storm Library, coz, if you need extra books for your investigations. Trust you two to find a murder to solve when you're supposed to be lying around eating honey cakes and gazing soulfully into each other's eyes.

Sorry to hear about Electra C, she was a good egg. Terrifying, obviously. One of those girls who can wither with a single sentence, never gave me the time of day when I was trying to be charming. But she was the one you'd want on your polo team, know what I mean? At least, you didn't want to be on the other team if she had a mallet in one hand, ha!

Your Bored in Boredville,
Henry

~

WIFE,

Do you think you could join me downstairs at the earliest convenient opportunity? We need to talk.

~

HUSBAND,

I'll be right down.

7

OUR SERVICES ARE NOT REQUIRED

*M*neme had not done anything wrong.

At least, she did not believe that she had done anything wrong. And yet, on her long walk from her dressing room to the parlour below, where her husband was waiting for her, a suspicion began to creep over her, that in fact her recent behaviour had been less than appropriate.

Surely not. She only wished to help with the investigation.

And in truth, she had hardly investigated at all. A discreet question or two to Juno, one of her dearest friends. A little private research into the magical hot spots of Aster, and the history of magical use on the island, thanks to the books she had sent for from Henry. And besides, that last might be entirely recreational research! Most of the references to magic on Aster turned out to be the same nonsense Phoebe Holiday had brought up — a myth about a beast with glowing eyes who roamed the hills and/or the moors hereabouts. Bunk, as Phoebe had suggested.

Certainly, Mneme had uncovered nothing of any

substance to be of use to the investigation of the murder of Mrs Electra Cheshire.

Yet, as Mneme hovered outside the door, there was a sinking feeling in her stomach. She had been married less than a fort-night and in all that time, she and Thornbury had not quarrelled. She knew that eventually, realities of the domestic would catch up with them and they would have to learn how to manage disagreements, but... still. This was their first. It would set the pattern for what was to follow.

One did not truly learn the measure of a person until you found out what rules they chose to abide by, when they were cross with someone they loved.

Mneme held her head high, and stepped into the room.

THORNBURY WAS ON THE COUCH, a book open on his lap. One of the books from the small shipment Cousin Henry had sent, Mneme realised. *Rural Magic and Rare Sightings* by Professor A.M. Witt — a whole chapter devoted to the mythical glowing-eyed beast of Aster, and barely a paragraph about how this island came to be magically null in the first place.

Mneme had learned a lot about Thornbury during their engagement. It had especially delighted her to discover that, for a professional man who was always so careful and precise in formal appearances, he was a careless reader. Put him near a pile of informative books and suddenly he would become a sprawling, unbuttoned creature. His shirt would become untucked, his limbs would flail, and he would almost always lose track of one of his shoes.

Had she not already been entirely in love with him, that endearing insight might well have pushed her over the precipice.

Perhaps today he had meant to sit straight-backed, ready to issue a reprimand to his wife. But as soon as the book lured him in, all formality had disappeared.

This Thornbury would be no trouble at all. Mneme should remember in future to always fill their marital home with strewn books.

"Husband," she greeted him politely. "Have you eaten?"

"Not yet." He placed the book aside, and immediately became the more formal version of himself, despite his skewed collar and unbuttoned cuffs. Thornbury's eyes fell gravely upon her. "Mneme."

"Yes, dear?"

"We are not to investigate the death of Mrs Electra Cheshire."

Poised to defend her own actions, she was not prepared for this particular tack. "If you mean that you do not wish me to interfere —"

He raised a hand solemnly. "If I wanted a wife who would not interfere with my investigations, I would not have married you, Mrs Seabourne."

That was... a reasonable statement. Entirely fair and from what she could tell, truthful.

Mneme huffed and went over to join him on the couch. If this was not to be a fight, she had no need to hold herself so aloof. "I only requested a few books from my cousin—"

"And combed Juno for gossip."

She gave him a stern look. "I don't *comb* people. And I won't ask how you knew about that."

Thornbury's hand found her thigh, and patted it in a

most familiar manner over the top of her summer muslin. "I should have explained the lie of the land to you before today. That's my fault. But despite my initial enthusiasm for assisting the local constabulary, we need to stay out of this one. Both of us."

"So we can enjoy our honeymoon?" she said in a small voice.

"Darling, I would happily solve ten murders with you if that was how you wished to spend our time together. But not this one."

"I don't understand," she pressed. "I'm sure Inspector Holiday is fine at his job. But look at who you are, what you do. This was a magical crime. Surely you are not going to entrust the investigation of your friend's mysterious death to the locals? Only a few days ago, you were so firm that you wished to see justice done."

Thornbury's hand stopped moving. His eyes looked troubled, an expression that Mneme wanted to entirely kiss away from him. Not yet, she told herself sternly. Facts before canoodling.

"The thing is," he said finally, after composing his thoughts. "Mrs Cheshire was my colleague, yes, once upon a time. I respected her professionally. And before that, we were students together. But it has been a very long time since I could honestly call her my friend."

Mneme blinked. There was a chill in his voice that was quite unfamiliar. "Then what was she to you?" she asked.

She did not expect his answer: "Professional rivals, at first. In recent years, she was my enemy. Or, at least, she considered me to be hers."

～

53

REVELATIONS like that deserved a strong cup of tea. Perhaps even a brandy. But they were currently without live-in domestic support, and Mneme would not pause this conversation for the world, even to ensure a cup of tea would be soon in her hands.

What she wouldn't give for a little magic right now, or a convenient valet to duck away and make refreshments for them. Still, she mustn't be ungrateful. Until now, she had greatly enjoyed the privacy of Comfrey Cottage, with a single visit from a quiet housekeeper every morning.

This particular conversation probably required privacy more than it required tea.

"Your enemy," Mneme repeated.

"Indeed," said Thornbury.

"I have so many questions."

"I expected as much."

"Does Inspector Holiday know this about you?"

"He believe so. I was informed this morning that my assistance would no longer be required on the case. If I am not currently the top of Holiday's suspect list, then he is a damned fool."

Mneme blinked, considering this. A *suspect*. Would she suspect her husband, if she were the one clodhopping around in Inspector Holiday's large boots?

Killing a person with magic on an island famously lacking in magic would certainly require specialised skills. Indeed, the small amount of useful information she had dredged from Henry's books suggested that the lack of magic on Aster was thanks to an ancient curse, or shielding spell, which meant that the person most equipped to bring about Mrs Cheshire's death must be a rather brilliant spell-cracker.

She had assumed thus far that Mrs Cheshire was an intimate friend from Thornbury's past, that the awkwardness between them at the Palace was perhaps due to a past romantic liaison, something neither he nor Henry had felt appropriate to disclose to her.

Until this moment, she had not considered the possibility that her husband might actually be the person who had killed Mrs Cheshire by the lake.

Thornbury gave a brief laugh, and cupped her cheek with his warm hand. "Mneme. Darling. I am excessively fond of your suspicious mind, and right now I can see it working quite furiously. Is there anything important you wish to ask me, before we continue this?"

For one moment, Mneme held her breath, imagining how he might answer the question that rose instantly on her tongue. *Did you kill her?*

Instead, what came out of her mouth, was another, almost as significant question. "Do you think we might have tea?"

Before, she did not want a pause in their conversation. Now, she wanted nothing more.

MOST SITUATIONS WERE DRASTICALLY IMPROVED with the addition of a hot cup of tea, even having to contemplate the possibility that one's husband might be a murder suspect.

Suspect, Mneme reminded herself. *Not the same as murderer.*

Her fancies were running away with her. As soon as her capable husband placed the teacup in her hand, she felt her nerves begin to settle. They sat at the kitchen table together, taking advantage of its utter emptiness. "You won't be arrested, will you?" she asked.

"That depends on what evidence is out there," Thornbury said, too calm for such a subject. "If the the murderer knows of my history with Electra, then it would be in their interest to make me look as guilty as possible."

That was a thought that even a cup of tea could not soften. Mneme set hers aside and moved from her chair into her husband's lap. It was not a manoeuvre she had attempted before, but the results were instantly pleasing; he caught hold of her and drew her close, the warmth of his body building against her light summer gown.

"I wish we'd never left these four walls," she murmured as he nuzzled at her throat. "Not for magical tea parties or rambles or Palace invitations. Can't we just stay indoors until our house is ready? Let the world out there solve all the murders."

"That is a most agreeable thought," said her husband, his hands drifting over her figure in an exploratory fashion. "But then, there is one invitation we cannot ignore."

Mneme groaned. The Midsummer Masque. "Must we? Won't she cancel it after everything? Mrs Cheshire was her social secretary. Surely the Queen is lost without her."

"You will find," said Thornbury, dipping his head low to kiss his way across her collar-bone. "Her Majesty will stop at nothing when she is set on an idea. A corpse or two is not going to stand in her way."

"But you have to go dressed as a donkey," Mneme wailed.

He laughed; and oh, that was one thing she had not entirely thought to expect of her new marriage. Here, in this house, in the magic-free and duty-free territory of this island, her new husband had become quite a merry soul. Even when under suspicion of murder. She was not sure she wanted him to go back to being constantly busy and exhausted from his work.

(The work, she might add, from which he was supposed to be mostly retired.)

"I don't mind the donkey head," Thornbury said. "Your costume is lovely, and I am looking forward to seeing you in it, dark fairy of mine."

They were, it seemed, to act out the tale of the midnight fairy tricked into loving a mortal who had been transformed into an ass. Mneme had been horribly relieved to learn that her costume was not also a joke played on them by the late Mrs Cheshire — or, if it was, that she was allowed to look pretty while others made fun.

Still, that donkey head annoyed her every time she walked past the cupboard where she had stashed it.

She shouldn't let that woman continue to get under her skin, especially considering that she was dead. Right now, they were alone in their honeymoon house, the masque was some days away, and she wanted to forget everything that existed outside these four walls.

"Really, Mr Seabourne? You're looking forward to seeing me in that gown? I thought you might prefer me out of this one." She shifted on his lap with a wicked smile, and was delighted to see her husband's eyes darken.

Thus far, their intimate moments outside the lovely bed upstairs had consisted of Thornbury pouncing, and Mneme quite happily being pounced upon. It was time, surely, for her to take a turn at pouncing. And it was, by all appearances, a remarkably sturdy chair...

8

CONVERSATIONS FOR THE
DRESSING ROOM

*B*umbleton Palace was enrobed for the occasion:
strung so heavily with bright lanterns that it
looked as though the cornices were on the verge of being
devoured by fairies.

Upon arrival, married women were separated from
their husbands and unmarried women were separated
from their mothers. Each guest, already costumed bril-
liantly, was ushered through a series of dressing rooms with
mirrors hung on every wall and door.

Mneme, who had spent the better part of an hour
pouring herself into the elaborate midnight fairy gown
(which had so many ribbons and satin cobwebs upon it
that she was not confident she would ever get out of it
again), felt that dressing rooms were somewhat unneces-
sary at this point. However, she spotted several young
ladies taking the opportunity to swap costumes, which
added somewhat to the evening's air of mischief and
merriment.

As a recently married lady, she was a little irritated at
being dragged away from her husband's company so soon.

She'd rather spend the evening at his side than anywhere else, even if he was disguised as an ass.

Being deprived of her husband's company, indeed, had been something of a pattern over the last several days. Since the death of Electra Cheshire, and the firm message from the local constabulary that he could not help with the investigation, Thornbury had thrown himself with a new and disturbing fervour into his hillwalking exercises, often skipping meals and returning in an irritable mood, windswept and exhausted. His attentions to his wife were as devoted as ever in the evenings, but his mind was elsewhere most of the time.

"Mneme! Finally. It's been an age."

A glamorous duchess swept across the dressing room, gowned in a bold, bright red gown covered in padded white hearts.

Only Juno would arrive at a queen's party dressed as a queen. She even held a sceptre, adorned with a soft red velvet heart to match those on her dress.

"Juno!" Mneme exclaimed in delight, embracing her friend. Despite the padding on her gown, and the impressive curves of her bosom, Juno looked thinner than usual, and tired beneath her powdered face. "I'm so glad to see you. Are you well? You needn't have come so far."

"Nonsense, the carriage ride over the bridge from Manticore was hardly bumpy at all. And I wasn't going to miss out on an invitation to Bumbleton Palace! This is the first event the Queen has held here since my wedding."

Sometimes Mneme forgot that before becoming the extravagantly marvellous Duchess of Storm, Juno had been a merry widow from a less renowned family, and thus had to exert effort to attract prestigious invitations. The idea of *wanting* party invitations had always been such anathema to Mneme that she regularly fell into the trap of assuming that, like herself, everyone would prefer to be at home with a good book.

"I am glad to see you," Mneme said honestly. Her friendship with Juno was barely a year old, but the other woman had become essential to her existence. "Shall we go through to the ballroom?"

Juno rolled her eyes. "You are like a newborn lamb at all this, aren't you? Your family name is quite wasted on you. Why would you leave the dressing rooms so swiftly at a royal event?"

"To attend the Midsummer Masque," Mneme said slowly. She pointed at the white, bejewelled mask on her face. It was already beginning to dig into her cheeks.

Juno tucked their arms together. "Nothing of any note will happen for hours yet. *This* is the place to be. In the dressing rooms, we speak of intimate things, so the dance floor and supper room can be reserved for empty subjects. The dressing rooms are where eternal friendships are forged and diplomatic battles are won. Also, we must find a maid to re-lace my slippers for me, because I get dizzy every time I lean over."

THERE WERE FOUR LADIES' dressing rooms in all. Mneme became acquainted with each in great detail thanks to Juno's insistence on a comprehensive promenade. So much for being slowed down by her delicate condition — Juno was more fired up than ever to suck the marrow out of every social event.

Mneme was able to offer Juno a few introductions, thanks to her recent appearance at the Queen's picnic. She had not yet spotted Lady Persimmon, or Mrs Phoebe Holiday, but she did stumble into a few royal aunties, and then Miss Wheaten, the reporter from *The Gentlewoman*.

Miss Wheaten went into raptures of delight at Juno's marvellous costume, and insisted she place her scarlet-and-gold mask on immediately, to be sketched by the team of urchins she had at the ready to produce fashion illustrations.

"Such a bore," said Juno afterwards, but she was glowing at the attention.

As they bid farewell to Miss Wheaten and her assistants, Mneme noticed a completed sketch sticking out of the satchel of one of the artists: a beribboned donkey head. "Look, Juno. Thornbury is already at the masque. I will *not* fuss about in here over shoes and gossip any longer."

"Such a wife you are," Juno teased her. "Oh, very well. I suppose a cup of ratafia fetched by my husband would taste better than anything they're serving in here. Let us arrive at the masque!"

Mneme readjusted her own mask so they could make their formal entrance.

An imposing older lady stood between the ladies and the main event, peering through a gilded mask-on-a-stick. She wore a tightly-boned, old fashioned gown with wide panniers, that had the air of being pulled from her own wardrobe rather than designed for this particular masque, and her towering white wig was practically vintage.

"And you would be?" she demanded, holding a clipboard of names.

Mneme remembered this lady: one of the ocean of aunties from the Queen's picnic. This one was an Edna or an Edith, though Mneme had forgotten her family name. She was helpful in assisting Mneme to find her stray husband on that day, though seemed less than friendly now.

"Nice to see you again, Lady —" she said politely. It was always wise to assume 'Lady' rather than 'Mrs' at this kind of event.

"Great Aunt Edith," bit out the older lady. Mneme should have remembered. The royal family members tended to ignore formal names around here, because they wished to emphasise their relationship to the Queen.

"Of course. I remember you from the tea party. May I introduce you to the Duchess of Storm. And I am —"

"I remember you also, Mrs Seabourne," Great Aunt Edith snapped, though she softened a little in the presence of a known duchess, giving Juno a polite head bob. "One of Mrs Cheshire's costume choices, I believe. The Midnight Fairy. An heirloom gown, most appropriate." She made a mark on the clipboard.

Behind them, Mneme head a few young ladies whispering in concern. They evidently had not realised there would be such tight security over who wore which costume, before they decided to switch.

"This would have been Mrs Cheshire's task, would it not?" Mneme asked. "Before her unfortunate…"

"I assure you I am quite capable of checking a list, Mrs Seabourne."

"Of course you are," Juno gushed. "I can just tell you're marvellous at the job already. How clever of you to step in."

Great Aunt Edith was not mollified by the flattery of a Duchess. "The role of social secretary was always earmarked for a close relative of the Queen, not an interloper from the city…"

"I quite agree." There was, Mneme had learned, a

power in agreeing with people, regardless of what they had to say.

Great Aunt Edith cast her eye over Juno's gown, taking in the bright scarlet fabric falling from just beneath the bust line, the merry white hearts, and the plunging neckline that quite emphasised the manner in which Juno's delicate condition had expanded her bosom. "The queen did not send you that costume, I think."

"I did not receive such an honour, madam," said Juno with a deference that made the older lady preen. "I found this old thing among my late mother-in-law's wardrobe, and wore it in her honour. Would you believe she wore it for the Old Queen's jubilee?"

Mneme did not believe in the least that such a daring and modern gown had been found anywhere but the sewing table of a contemporary dressmaker, and she could tell that Great Aunt Edith was not convinced either. Still, they must have sufficiently buttered her up, as she made a tick against Juno's name.

"Very fashionable, the late Duchess of Storm," Great Aunt Edith muttered.

"I try to live up to her reputation, every day," Juno agreed gleefully, sweeping Mneme past the Queen's new social secretary, into the Midsummer Masque.

Mneme had no idea where in the palace they were; it felt like another world. The walls were lined with trees that dripped with gold, silver and jewels. Lanterns swayed from above, casting the eerie effect of false moonlight.

For all Juno's protestations that the ball would not properly 'begin' for hours yet, the festivities were certainly underway: dancing couples swooped by, and all manner of masked faces loomed at them through the shadows.

"How will I ever find Thornbury in this?" Mneme complained.

"There can't be many donkeys in attendance," said Juno, as two gentlemen dressed like a bear and a fox walked past them. "Goodness. Turns out, your husband is more fashionable than either of us."

"Stranger things have happened," said Mneme.

"Not in the entire history of the world, my dear."

A goddess leaped at them, out from the nearby supper room. She wore a fierce golden mask, a swirling white gown, and winged sandals upon her feet. "Mrs Seabourne," she said, her body shaking with what looked very much like fury. "Where is your husband?"

"I haven't the least idea," said Mneme, blinking at the woman whom she only now recognised as Lady Persimmon Manticore. Her long dark hair was braided tonight, falling in long, beaded plaits to her waist. "Can I help you with something?"

"He won't get away with this," growled Lady Persimmon and tore off through the crowd. Gold feathers fluttered behind her as she pushed past various merrymakers.

Mneme watched her go. "Should we follow?"

"I'd lay odds on her finding Thornbury before you do," agreed Juno, turning Mneme about so the two of them could pursue the vengeful goddess. "Really, such manners. You're supposed to pretend not to recognise people, at a party like this."

"That was Lady Persimmon Manticore," Mneme informed her.

"Oh, I've met her before. She was at my wedding."

"She was?" Mneme had attended Henry and Juno's wedding herself, which was sparsely attended due to a recent family scandal. She did not remember the brooding presence of Lord Manticore and she certainly did not recall making the acquaintance of Lady Persimmon.

"Oh, they didn't stay. The Queen sent Lord and Lady Manticore as her representatives, to deliver a private message of congratulations before the ceremony. One has to expect that sort of thing, when one marries into a duchy. I liked the wife — quiet but sharp, you know? Someone who notices things. I enjoy that in people."

"Yes," said Mneme heavily. Noticing things. Like how Lady Persimmon had clearly noticed all the favours heaped upon her own husband by the young Queen who was enamoured of him.

"Ooh, that sounds like gossip," said Juno. "Put a pin in it for later. I've spotted your ass!"

Up ahead, they could indeed see that familiar beribboned donkey head, worn by a man in well-tailored breeches, and a long gold-and-green coat that Mneme did not recognise. The man in the mask was pinned against a wall, between an ornamental jewel tree and a punch table. He was, however, too tall and broad of shoulder to be Thornbury.

Lady Persimmon had the man hemmed in, speaking in a heated manner.

"… will not let his father take Eddie away from us," she said, before realising there were witnesses. She gave Juno and Mneme a fierce, scorching glare from beneath her golden mask, then turned back to the donkey. "Do something about it," she commanded, and then marched away.

Juno and Mneme glanced at each other.

"What was all that about?" Juno asked.

The man in the donkey mask hesitated, then attempted a shrug.

Mneme rolled her eyes. "You're not going to convince me you're my husband by staying quiet," she informed him. "You're the wrong shape."

The donkey head bobbed in acceptance. Its wearer

reached up to remove the heavy false head, revealing a tousle-headed and slightly sweaty Duke of Storm. "What ho," said Henry faintly. "It's my two favourite ladies. How's tricks?"

INSTEAD OF ONE formal supper room, the Midsummer Masque featured several small supper alcoves, each decorated to a different theme. Juno, Mneme and Henry found a tiny bower full of sugared macarons and fish paste crackers (underwater theme: paper seaweed and octopus tentacles hanging from the ceiling) which was otherwise empty. They crowded in together, tugging the curtain closed for a semblance of privacy.

"What is Thornbury up to?" Mneme demanded.

"Can't a fellow borrow another fellow's donkey head without their wives making unwarranted assumptions about…" Henry began.

Juno clicked her tongue impatiently.

"Oh, I don't know. He said something about necessary discretion and needing to avoid scrutiny. I'm retired from such shenanigans," Henry added, sounding slightly put out. "I'm sure he'll fill me in later."

Thornbury had certainly better be prepared to explain it all Mneme, if he knew what was good for him.

"What was Lady Manticore talking about?" Juno pressed.

"I haven't the faintest!" Henry insisted. "She wanted to talk about Electra's boy, gawd knows why."

"Electra's boy. Eddie, I presume?" asked Mneme, thinking it over. Freddy, Alfie and Ed. Those were the boys that Lady Persimmon had with her, when they met Phoebe for tea, and at the Queen's picnic. A horde of scamps, clearly well-loved and inseparable. One of the boys was fairer of hair colour and complexion than the others. Did Lady Persimmon and Mrs Cheshire share a nursemaid? Certainly they were close friends, based on Lady Persimmon's grief at losing her.

"That's right!" said Henry. "I looked up our old Delphi College pics, after I wrote to you. Edmund Cheshire, he married Electra, and then came a cropper with some curse or other years later. Here on Aster, actually, doing some experiments about magic or not magic or whatever. Only Edmund could get himself blown up by a curse on an island with no magic. The boy was barely born at the time — or maybe he came after? There was no Season that year — mouse plague, you know — and when all the social thingummies started up again, there was Electra back at Court as if nothing had ever happened. And also, you know, not at Court." He did some kind of wink-wink-nudge-nudge gesture that made Mneme wonder all over again how he had possibly held down a double life as a secret agent for so long. "Secret business. They didn't put us on the same missions very often because she found me annoying, and she could wrap the old man around her little finger, always got the jobs she wanted."

By old man, Mneme assumed he meant Octavian Swift, the spymaster.

"Lady P mentioned little Eddie's father," said Juno. "Did she mean Edmund Cheshire is back from the dead, or that someone else fathered her child?"

"No idea," said Henry cheerfully. "None of my business who's bedding who, as long as there's no treason involved. No gossip here, only snacks." He ate a fish paste cracker.

"It's my business if she's pulling my husband into it," said Mneme. "Why on earth would Lady Persimmon think that Thornbury had any say in the custody of Mrs Cheshire's child?"

"Well," said Juno, moving away from her husband as he attempted to give her a fish paste kiss on the cheek. "There's only one way to find out that information, my dear. You must ask your husband."

"Have to find him first," said Henry, and promptly received twin glares from his wife, and his cousin. "I say, what did I say?"

9

MOONLIT SIGHTINGS OF LOCAL
FAUNA

*A*ccording to Henry, Mr C. Thornbury Seabourne was currently wearing the mask of a cat, and a splendid pair of over-sized boots to go with the swapped costume. Mneme set off to find her husband, leaving Juno and Henry behind to bicker about how unseemly it was for a Duke to dress as a donkey in public, even in the name of friendship and national security.

Away from the main ballroom, where the gilded trees and shadowed crowds and dancing made it quite impossible to find anyone, the party bled out into the rest of the palace. Mneme found flirting couples arranged on every staircase, and giggling young ladies darting back and forth from the dressing rooms, still trying to evade the disapproval of Great Aunt Edith and her mighty clipboard.

According to a wine-soaked gentleman leaning on a priceless painting, some fellow in a silver coat with the mask of a cat and a pair of excessively large boots had passed him a little while ago, heading for the Moonlight Gallery.

Mneme remembered how to get there, at least, though

she shuddered at the thought of visiting that disturbing exhibit at night-time.

Her thoughts had become quite chaotic. She had to assume that Lady Persimmon was determined to raise Mrs Cheshire's son along with her own. The most obvious assumption, based on how so many aristocratic families handled these matters, was that Lord Manticore was the natural father of the boy, and Lady Persimmon had taken him into her household out of convenience, and loyalty to her husband.

That might explain, at least, why Mrs Cheshire had fallen out of favour with the Queen enough to be exiled to the country a few years ago, but not why the Queen kept her so close at hand here at Bumbleton Palace, nor why Lady Persimmon and Mrs Cheshire seemed to be such intimate friends.

Besides, if Lord Manticore were the natural father, then there would be no reason Lady Persimmon might think Ed's father was going to take him away from her family…

Certainly no reason why she might believe Thornbury would have any influence over the matter, of all people.

The one possibility Mneme would *not* dwell upon was that her own husband might be the boy's natural father — she suspected from the look Juno gave her as they parted that her friend had entertained such a thought, however briefly. But no, Thornbury had many secrets in his professional life that Mneme did not expect him to ever share with her, but something of such domestic significance as a child — he would have told her before they married. He was too painfully honest not to admit such a connexion.

Henry, of course, might be a potential candidate to have fathered the boy. He was at least slightly rakish before settling down with Juno, even now that Mneme knew that most of his public silliness was a cover for his secret government work. Everyone knew that Thornbury was the best person to consult if you wished to influence the Duke of Storm. But if young Ed was part-Seabourne, there was no way he would have preserved that bright head of blond hair instead of the red-gold that her family had resigned themselves to, generation after generation.

Mneme had now reached the Moonlight Gallery. Unlike her first visit to this strange exhibit of costumes, masks and theatrical oddities, the curtains were all tied open. The glass-walled gallery was flooded with bright moonlight, illuminating every nook and plinth.

Standing at the windows, his back to the gallery and his face firmly turned towards the equally moonlit palace grounds, she saw Lord Manticore. It could not be anyone else. He wore the fur robes of an ancient warrior, his dark hair looped and braided. If he wore a mask it was a small piece, only covering his face, and she could not see it.

There was no reason Mneme should not be in this part of the palace, and yet she was struck with an overwhelming sensation that she should not be here. There was no Thornbury, in any case, so lurking in the doorway was probably a waste of her time. She turned away... and then, sensing movement in the gallery behind her, turned back for a moment.

A figure in bright white robes, wearing a grotesque parody of a donkey mask on his head, rose up behind Lord Manticore, holding a large bronze sword that gleamed in the searing moonlight.

Mneme screamed, too late to stop the blow.

10

A SURFEIT OF DONKEYS

*A*fterwards, Mneme would swear she had not fainted. She only blinked her eyes, to recover her sensibilities. Not only from witnessing the death of Lord Manticore…

After she screamed, the man in the hideous donkey mask ran directly at her with that gleaming bronze sword, and then, and then… something swept her aside to safety. Something dark, with glowing eyes.

Panic and horror and confusion swept over her…

When she blinked her eyes open again, the Moonlight Gallery was full of people, and Mnemosyne Seabourne was on the ground.

It was possible there might have been a tiny bit of a swoon. But definitely not a faint. She was a hardened adventurer, and she drew the line at fainting.

A cat-faced man in a gold-and-green coat lurched over her, and Mneme cried out in alarm.

Glowing eyes emerging from the shadows, reflecting the sharp moonlight…

"Oh, Henry, honestly!" complained Juno, snapping Mneme back to reality.

The silver cat mask slid off to reveal, once again, Mneme's slightly shamefaced cousin, his bright red-gold hair rumpled.

"Why are you wearing that," Mneme protested. "Why."

"Swapped back with Thornbury," said Henry cheerfully. "He's the ass now. Haven't you seen him? He was downstairs a moment ago."

There was a cluster of nobles and palace guards over by the window, where Lord Manticore's lifeless body might even now be…

"…perfectly fine," Juno was explaining. "Something of a bump on his head, of course."

"Lucky escape, really," Henry agreed.

Mneme blinked several more times and thankfully, this time there were no more alarming blackouts. "Is Lord Manticore *alive?*"

"Someone attacked him," Juno explained. "I thought you were a witness! Didn't you see?"

"Part of it." There was no excuse for not recalling every detail, not with the moonlight that flooded the room, illuminating every creepy mask and mannequin. "I saw something," Mneme managed slowly. "I saw…" *A beast with glowing eyes and black pointed ears like a cat…* "The other donkey mask," she managed. "Not Thornbury's. The one from the display."

Lady Persimmon was over there, she realised, helping her husband to his feet. Lord Manticore looked dazed but he wasn't even bleeding.

"There was a sword," Mneme went on. She knew there had been a sword. Why was there no blood?

"Fascinating, darling," said Juno, squeezing her hand.

73

"But I do think you'd better save it for that nice Inspector fellow, he's the one asking all the questions."

Inspector Holiday, his face set in a rather less kindly expression than he had worn at the scene of Mrs Cheshire's murder, approached Mneme from the other side of the gallery. "Ah, Mrs Seabourne," he said sternly. "Now, what's all this about a donkey?"

~

Juno did not leave Mneme's side, for which Mneme was quite grateful. She still felt faint, which was embarrassing, and she was extremely concerned about the lack of Thornbury. Surely he would have heard by now that a crime had taken place. Why was he not in the thick of it, like Henry?

Henry had put himself at the Inspector's disposal, relaying information back and forth between the Inspector and the Queen, who had apparently summoned her private physician to treat Lord Manticore in her rooms, and was refusing to leave his side — an awkward situation, to be sure. Her Majesty's burning attachment to Lord Manticore was on display for all to see, and no one at the palace seemed remotely surprised by it.

Mneme did her best to explain what she had seen — and to clarify that the donkey mask worn by Lord Manticore's attacker was quite a different beast (so to speak) than the one her husband and Henry had swapped back and forth that evening.

She did not hesitate until the Inspector asked her what had happened after the attacker fled the scene. "Someone pulled me out of the way," she admitted.

"Another witness!" the Inspector crowed, making a note of it. "Did you recognise the fellow?"

"He wore a mask," Mneme said. "Black — like a cat? With, uh. Bright eyes."

A magical creature on an island devoid of magic.

The Inspector made a note of her description, but there was a frown on his face now, like he could tell that she was not being entirely truthful… or that it was not something he wished to hear. "What other rooms are on this floor? No one reported a black masked man or a donkey with a sword on the staircase."

"Six bedrooms, a poetry library and a planetarium," said Henry crisply. "Your capable wife, Mrs Holiday, is supervising the search of those rooms with some of the ladies. I sent some guards with them in case there are any surprises along the way."

"Excellent," said Inspector Holiday, looking quietly proud. "No one like my Phoebe for ferreting out clues."

"We found something, dear!"

Mrs Phoebe Holiday, leading a phalanx of maids and aunties, returned to the Moonlight Gallery holding a bright bronze sword, which she held out to her husband. She had used a handkerchief to wrap the hilt, as if she thought that the thing might be cursed. "It's not sharp at all," Phoebe reported. "A theatre prop, I believe? But quite hefty. I think it might be what the attacker used to whack Lord Manticore over the head. Found it in the Beige Bedroom."

"And we found these, Inspector," said Great Aunt Edith, looking a little too triumphant. "Near an open window in the poetry library." She emptied out a beige pillowcase which contained — Mneme gasped — a familiar donkey head mask covered in ribbons, and the same silver-and-white coat that Thornbury had been wearing when they set out that evening.

"That's the chap," said Inspector.

"No," Mneme insisted. "That isn't the same mask at all. There was another in the collection… Mrs Cheshire showed it to me on the day of the picnic." But Mrs Cheshire, of course, was not here to corroborate her story. "King Osbert used to wear it to chase maids around the palace," she said plaintively.

"Well, really! Such scurrilous rumourmongering," said Great Aunt Edith, looking highly offended. "Inspector Holiday, I can assure you there is only one donkey mask in the palace catalogue, and it was signed out to Mr Thornbury Seabourne for tonight's occasion." She produced her clipboard as proof

"Was it now," said Inspector Holiday, stroking his chin. "Seabourne, you say? Sounds like it might be time to arrest the fellow."

≈

THORNBURY WAS NOT ARRESTED that night, but only because no one in Bumbleton Palace could find him.

≈

MNEME WAS OFFERED a palace bedroom by a helpful maid, but she could not imagine sleeping a wink. Juno and Henry had taken over the job of loudly professing to Inspector Holiday that Thornbury, if he could not be found, was either investigating the attack on Lord Manticore, or had somehow fallen afoul of the real attacker.

Great Aunt Edith, speaking with all the authority she could muster as the Queen's social secretary (quite a lot, as it happened) maintained that Thornbury was clearly the main suspect.

Mneme slipped away from all the chaos, finally, and

found refuge in the poetry library where, by all accounts, her husband had removed his coat and disappeared into the night. She took off her mask and sank into an armchair to think and doze.

There was moonlight here too, though it streamed into the library at a different angle, not quite so fierce and all-encompassing as in the Moonlight Gallery.

Finally, at some time past four in the morning, the enormous moon set and darkness properly fell over the palace, just in time for dawn to start smudging its way over the horizon. The sunrises and sunsets were both especially colourful on the Isle of Aster, probably because of the magic-free air. Mneme had not witnessed a sunrise here before, because she had not quite found the strength to roll out of her honeymoon bed as early as her husband was wont to do. Perhaps she would have the leisure to watch this one, as she fretted about the situation.

She missed her magic. She might have a dozen ways to contact her missing husband, if her magic was warm beneath her skin. She had never felt so empty and useless in her whole life.

A Seabourne without magic was… just a person.

"Thornbury," Mneme murmured. "Where are you?"

There was a sound; a soft thump, like a cat landing on a roof. Only it came from below the window. The trellis creaked. Someone nearby caught his breath.

She did not think to be afraid, not with an Inspector and his investigators (and Henry, always more useful than he appeared) half a shout away. Instead, she felt terribly calm, and terribly curious.

A dark shape came over the window sill, and a body landed on the soft carpet.

Mneme, who had not done so before now, leaned over

and struck the convenient tinder that lay by the nearest lamp, and lit the oil. It sizzled, just a little.

Thornbury, rumpled and coatless, crouched on the carpet, blinking at her. He still wore the same shirt and breeches he had arrived in, though they looked much the worse for wear. He also looked… not quite right. He was blinking too much in the lamplight, staring at her like he did not entirely recognise his wife.

"Where have you been?" Mneme demanded. "They think you tried to kill Lord Manticore. What have you got there?"

Her heart sank as her husband uncurled from around the object he held; another beige pillowcase, containing something very large. As she watched, he emptied it out on the floor: a hideous, grotesque mask made from the severed head of a donkey.

11

WHATEVER HAPPENED TO MR CHESHIRE?

*M*neme reacted quickly, kicking the donkey head so that it rolled under the nearest armchair. Thornbury blinked at her. "What was that for?"

"You're likely to be arrested," she told him. "Very soon."

He nodded, utterly unsurprised. "Electra."

"No," said Mneme from between gritted teeth. "For attacking Lord Manticore with a fake sword. Whomever did it wore that mask."

"I found it outside. Someone chucked it out a window. Is he all right?" Thornbury asked, his throat rasping as if it were very dry.

Mneme was not about to call a maid to bring him refreshments, but she could not sit by and let her husband speak with a sore throat. Not when every good poetry library came with a drinks cabinet.

Quietly, she poured him a small measure of brandy, and handed it over so that he might answer the many, many questions bursting up inside of her.

"I'll answer yours if you answer mine," she said, bouncing with impatience.

Thornbury sipped, waving her to continue.

Mneme outlined the details of the attack on Lord Manticore in the Moonlight Gallery. Unlike her report to the Inspector, she did not hold back from the description of the strange, dark creature with glowing eyes.

Thornbury nodded, recovering some of his usual poise as he reached the bottom of the ratafia glass. "Sounds about right. Manticore had a lucky escape."

"Meanwhile," Mneme said tartly. "You are a wanted man, so if you could hurry up with your side of the explanations? Where have you been all night?"

"I spent a great part of it in the miraculous gazebo," said Thornbury, setting the glass aside.

"Why on earth?"

"I received a message from an old friend, who I thought might shed some light on our local mystery."

Mneme frowned. "By mystery, do you mean, Mrs Cheshire's death?"

"I mean, the use of quite advanced magic in order to fake the death of Mrs Cheshire. And to put that damned gazebo there, actually, so it's two mysteries I was looking to solve."

Mneme gasped at the first revelation, ignoring the second. One thing at a time, and her interest level in gazebo installations was negligible. "Mrs Cheshire is alive?"

"I expect so," said Mr Thornbury, looking thoroughly exasperated. "She's the one who sent me the note tonight. I'm fairly sure she's also the one who sent an anonymous message to the Inspector, detailing all the reasons why I could not be trusted in the investigation of her death. Only Electra could be that petty."

Fascinated now, Mneme held out a hand to raise her husband from the floor, so he might sit more comfortably in an armchair. "So who did we find by the lake, if that wasn't Mrs Cheshire's body?"

"I have no idea," Thornbury said, frowning as he always did, when there was a puzzle to be solved. "Either it was a long-lasting illusion on some other body, or it was Electra herself, charmed to look completely dead. Either way, it involved far more magic than you would be able to perform even in one of the small magical pockets on this island. Whoever performed that spell had access to a mobile source of magic that defies the island's own curse."

Mneme sighed. "You've — been missing for the whole night because you've been trying to solve this problem, haven't you? You realise that tonight's note was probably intended to get you out of the way exactly so that you could be blamed for Lord Manticore's attack?"

"Doesn't surprise me," said Thornbury. "Blaming me for her crimes is Electra's modus operandi, going right back to school."

Mneme gave him a steady look. "Speaking of which…"

He winced. "What more is there?"

"Does Lady Persimmon Manticore know that Mrs Cheshire is not dead?"

"No idea. They've been thick as thieves for years, might have cooked up the scheme together."

"Lady Persimmon was looking for you tonight. Gave Henry an earful about the custody of Mrs Cheshire's son."

An expression of inexpressible awkwardness cross her husband's face. "Ah. That."

"Anything you want to tell me?"

"You don't think —"

"It's been a very long night, darling, why don't you just

assume that I want to know every single detail. Leave nothing out."

Thornbury held his glass out hopefully. Mneme took it from him and gave him a half measure of brandy. He would have more than that when he had earned it.

"Electra Cheshire was the subject of some rather scurrilous rumours, shortly before her exile," said Thornbury. "Firstly, that her son had not been fathered by her late husband. Secondly, that the natural father was — someone rather high up in her Majesty's government. She was not transferred away from Town because of that — but no one knew the real reason, so it was assumed the Queen sent her here as a kindness to escape the gossip and protect her child. With her magical abilities, this island must have felt like a prison."

"Who is the father?" Mneme asked.

"I believe the boy is my brother," said Thornbury, eyes fixed on hers.

"Oh." She hadn't thought of that at all. Octavian Swift, the Queen's spymaster. Given how little involvement he had in Thornbury's own upbringing, until his son was old enough to contribute to the family business, it seemed odd that he would take an interest in little Ed now. "Lady Persimmon seemed to think you would have influence over Ed's father," she realised.

"I'd volunteer us to adopt the child ourselves if it would free him from Swift," said Thornbury. "But I believe we'd have to queue for the privilege. And of course, Electra would rather die than have me involved in Eddie's life."

"Assuming she's not dead already."

"Assuming that, yes."

"But why would Mrs Cheshire choose to fake her own death in the first place?" Mneme burst out. "And what has this to do with the attack on Lord Manticore tonight?"

"For that, I believe we need to ask questions of a wider circle of people," said Thornbury. "Starting with Lady Manticore."

"Why her in particular?" Mneme asked.

"Convenience, mostly," said her husband, with a wry twist of his mouth. He nodded his head towards a nearby bookshelf full of antique poetry volumes. "She's standing over there."

FOR A MOMENT THE ILLUSION HELD: one standing set of bookshelves among many. But as Mneme stared, actually paying attention to something other than her husband, she saw a telltale flicker at the edges of the wood. The almost imperceptible hum of magic. No wonder she had been drawn to this room more than any other on this floor of the palace: this was another magical pocket, well hidden.

The illusion broke open, and Lady Persimmon Manticore stepped into the room, her expression somewhere between menacing and miserable. She had abandoned her mask and winged sandals but still wore her white costume gown.

(White, the person who attacked Lord Manticore was wearing white, but Mneme could have sworn it was a different style of robes.)

"Lady Manticore," said Thornbury politely. "How is your husband? I'm surprised you left his side tonight."

"He has all the comfort he needs," said Persimmon. "How did you know about this?" She gestured behind her, at the false bookshelf.

"I rather have the advantage, when it comes to finding

cracks in the island's shield against magic," said Thornbury, sounding almost apologetic. "I'm the one who put them there."

There were no teacups or hedgehogs immediately to hand; Mneme threw a cushion at him.

"That's fair," he conceded, wincing in her general direction. "Sorry, love."

"Why would you not tell me?"

"Because, of course, it was a secret," he sighed. "If I spent our honeymoon confessing all the secrets I know, we would have no time for anything else."

"But the Isle of Aster's lack of magic is a shield, you say. Not a curse?"

"King Osbert had it installed, several reigns ago. He was paranoid about being assassinated by magic."

Persimmon raised both her eyebrows. "And how did he die?"

"Poisoned dart to the neck," admitted Thornbury.

"Chased one too many maids?" Mneme muttered.

"Certainly made a miscalculation about the last one he chased," Thornbury agreed. "Anyway, when Queen Aud came to the throne, she had Lord Manticore installed as her Advisor on Magical Matters, and he immediately called attention to the danger of having the royal country residence devoid of magic. Called in a team to do something about it — create some loopholes in the shield that only the Queen and her protectors would know about."

"And you were on that team," Mneme guessed.

"Not officially. Edmund Cheshire was the one who put the team together. He wanted me for my spellcracking ability, but I was already working for my father, as was Electra. Cheshire requested that the Queen's Consultant lend us to his team."

"So," said Persimmon, giving him a searing look of

disapproval. "You were there. You know what happened to Electra's Edmund."

"I know that he told us the intention was to create three small, controllable pockets of magic in an island completely shielded by magic," said Thornbury, sounding calm, though his hands shook a little. "Later, we figured out that he was planning something rather more ambitious — an attempt to remove the entire shield from the island. But by the time we realised what he was doing, it was already in motion. The spells were solid, the procedures were immaculate. But everything went wrong. We cracked the shield all over the island — wild, erratic holes burst through the shield. To this day, there are still some we never managed to catalogue. Most of them are stable — the tea room by the lake, the bookshelf behind you. Many are not. There's one, for instance, up on the moors that moves four inches due west every full moon. And another that... well. Moves independently, one might say."

Mneme needed an entire tea tray to deal with this. Not only hot tea in a porcelain cup. She needed a mountain of buttered scones. Possibly some grilled kippers. If high tea became higher the later it got into the evening, then what kind of tea was appropriate an hour or so before dawn, when one's husband was confessing more secrets than could possibly fit into a single marriage?

She deserved bacon and eggs, at the very least.

"Is that why you've spent so many hours wandering around the countryside since we got here?" she asked. "Have you been investigating an old case?" His need for fresh air had got even more intensive, she realised, after Electra's death was revealed. But he had been doing it all along...

Thornbury looked mildly guilty. "I did invite you to join me," he reminded her. "Every time."

She was going to need that cushion back, to scream into. "Thornbury, you have to tell me all the facts. Every time. I thought you were on *holiday*."

"Is this how you think Electra pulled off her deception?" Lady Persimmon asked, in a smaller and altogether less accusatory voice than before. "Using that — portable pocket of magic?"

"Ah," said Thornbury, sympathy creeping into his tone. "I see she didn't tell you about her plan."

"I can't think why she did it."

"I can."

Both women stared at him with varying degrees of impatience.

Thornbury gave a great sigh and rose to his feet. "Mrs Seabourne," he said, extending his hand to his wife. "Would you care to take a walk on the nearby hillside? I believe I can show you the answer to all of your questions."

"I'll need better footwear," said Mneme.

"I'll find you some," said Lady Persimmon. "I'm coming too."

DAWN ROSE over Bumbleton Palace as Mr and Mrs Seabourne hiked away from it: up and over the surrounding hills in the company of a sensibly-booted Lady Persimmon Manticore. The wind was indeed rather sharp this early in the morning. Mneme was glad she had found a shawl as well as borrowed boots for this particular expedition.

"You said Electra wasn't sent to Bumbleton Palace because of the scandal about her son," she said, in a quiet voice to her husband. Lady Persimmon was walking a little apart from them, head up, maintaining her pride. "But you know why she was exiled from Town?"

"Oh yes," said Thornbury, also in a quiet voice so that Lady Persimmon might not hear. "She was dropped from the secret service because she tried to kill an agent she was partnered with. Even Octavian Swift couldn't let that one go. The Queen pardoned her, but she couldn't work with us again. The Bumbleton Palace job was a convenience and a punishment all at once."

"She tried to —" Mneme gave him a startled look, which her husband met with a twisted sort of grin. "Oh, it was you, wasn't it?"

"To be fair, she was convinced I was a traitor at the time. But everyone already knew of her dislike for me, so she didn't come out of it smelling like roses." He looked resigned, and a little sad. "Around that time, she found out my true connexion to Swift, and realised that our professional rivalry had never been fair. Regardless how hard she worked, what a brilliant agent she was… even having borne his child. He would never take her side over mine."

Mneme considered this. "If you had been a traitor, you probably would have got away with it."

Thornbury nodded. "Don't think I haven't had my offers. I am a source of great frustration to nearly every government on the Continent."

She tucked her arm in his. "I sympathise with them greatly, my dear. You are also a great source of frustration to your wife."

1 2

A LAIR WITH A VIEW

*I*t took them around half an hour's elevated stroll to reach Mrs Cheshire's invisible lair.

"And you knew it was here all along?" Mneme asked her husband, managing somehow to keep reproach out of her voice. (That was for a more private conversation, to be conducted when all of this was over. She had several items saved up for that conversation already, but she would allow herself the indulgence of including them all.)

"This was where we worked together when we tried to break the shield," he admitted. "There was a hideout here then, and it's one of the few magical pockets that no one knows about."

Mneme examined the empty space. It flickered a little, from time to time. A tell-tale sign of invisibility. No one would notice from a distance. This pocket was powerful indeed — she could feel her own magic sparking, coming alive, even at a distance. That had not happened in the Bumbleton Palace magical pocket, or at the Blue Butter-cup, not until she was inside the magical field.

Thornbury stood straighter. Clearly the magic was

affecting him, too. "It has the same magical signature as that damned gazebo," he said in a considering voice.

Lady Persimmon gave him a suspicious look. "You can read magical signatures in a non-magical environment?"

Mneme could not help but feel smug about her husband's abilities. And to think, her mamma believed her to have married beneath her!

"It takes some patience," said Thornbury. "A whisper rather than a shout, especially once the original source of the magic has gone."

"So," said Mneme, just to be sure she had her facts straight. "Someone lured you to the gazebo with a suspicious note to get you out of the way, and once you were there, you waited *hours* longer than necessary, because you were distracted by the mystery of how it was built in the first place."

Thornbury looked rather abashed. "More evidence that Electra is pulling all the strings. Whomever sent that note knew me rather too well."

"Don't mind me," Mneme said airily. "I'm absorbing so much information on how to manage you, once we have a home of our own."

Lady Persimmon pouted at the shimmering veil of invisibility before them: barely noticeable unless you knew what to look for, that not-quite-realness of the apparently empty space. "Electra!" she cried aloud. "Open up this instant. What do you think you are doing?"

The invisibility veil shivered for a moment, and then a bright green door appeared. Persimmon knocked on it with her fists. "Electra!" she shouted again.

"For goodness sake," said an impatient voice as the door was flung open to reveal the sour-faced Mrs Cheshire, in a dressing gown and slippers, her golden hair in a rumpled net for sleeping. "Sound travels in the hills, you know!"

"You wretch," sobbed Lady Persimmon, and flung herself into Mrs Cheshire's arms.

Electra Cheshire cradled her friend tenderly, and shot a poisonous glare at Thornbury and Mneme over Lady Persimmon's heaving shoulder. "Oh good," she said sarcastically. "Exactly the couple I would have invited for breakfast."

THEY ATE on a balcony in the sunshine, overlooking Bumbleton Palace while remaining concealed from sight from outside thanks to the veil of invisibility.

Breakfast was fruit and pastries and hot, perfect tea, heated with magic as was only right and proper. Mneme had been telling herself she must be quiet, observe, not interrupt with her usual fuss of questions, but actually now the tea was here, she was more than happy to be a spectator to this scene.

It became clear within thirty seconds of seeing them together in this private space that Electra and Persimmon were more than bosom friends: they were lovers. Persimmon's fury at Electra's betrayal was fierce enough to burn down the surrounding hills, and a generous spread of breakfast foods and hot tea was not enough to distract her from her righteous anger.

It did not smooth matters at all when, upon seating himself at the table, the first thing Thornbury said was: "And are we expecting Edmund to join us this morning?"

This earned him another vicious glare from Mrs Cheshire, who gritted her teeth and replied: "He comes and he goes as he wills."

Lady Persimmon banged her cup against her saucer. "Electra, is — is your husband alive? Did you make this hidden home with him?" She sounded like her heart was breaking.

"It's not like that, darling," Electra promised her. "It's far more complicated. If I could only explain —"

"Why yes, I do believe I am owed an explanation. You faked your own death, Electra. How could you possibly put me through that? The children, *Eddie*. How could you make us think —" Lady Persimmon buried her face in a cloth napkin, sobbing quietly.

Electra Cheshire looked quite pale, possibly feeling a rare stab of guilt. "It wasn't supposed to be like this at all," she assured Persimmon. "It was the only way I could see out of the mess I was in."

"I saw your corpse," hissed Persimmon. "On a hillside. Wearing boots that I bought you."

"I know, and I'm so sorry." Electra took her hand and, amazingly, Persimmon allowed her to do so. "The last few years with have been the best of my life. I thought we were safe here. But — you know who Eddie's father is now, I think."

"I worked it out," said Persimmon in an icy voice. "He came to our house and threatened me. Octavian Swift, Queen's Consultant. In my house. The house of her Majesty's favourite minister, as if our family's power meant nothing to us. He wants to take Ed away."

"I didn't think he would do that," said Electra. "I never thought he cared enough to try."

Thornbury cleared his throat. "Electra, what has Swift threatened? It must be bad to have forced you to this level of desperation."

Electra turned a most scathing expression upon him. "Honestly, Thornbury, you're supposed to be clever. Faking

91

my own death had nothing to do with Swift. I might not be an agent any more, but I am still the Queen's woman. Here in the country — where she is most vulnerable — I am the person closest to her. With war brewing on the Continent, and approximately twelve different foreign marriage proposals in current negotiation with our Queen… do you really think the pressures that drove me to desperation were *internal*?"

"Oh," said Thornbury, recalculating. "You've had offers?"

"I have had threats," she hissed. "Credible threats. Against my son, against my love and her children." She rolled her eyes at Persimmon. "Even against my love's husband, who was foolish enough to think no one would notice that he and the Queen are embroiled in the most preposterous exchange of mutual pining. Pull one thread and the Teacup Isles will fall into a mess of scandal and diplomatic disasters. I had to take myself off the board."

Having said her piece, Electra turned back to sweet-talk Persimmon. "Darling, it wasn't supposed to happen this way. I always intended to discuss it with you before I staged my death, and to have a plan in place for Ed's custody. I've been gathering a portfolio of evidence that my son was fathered by Edmund before his death. My will was to be changed, to give you the first rights of adoption."

"So what went wrong?" Lady Persimmon asked, her voice shaking with quiet rage. "How can you possibly justify what you put us through?"

Electra faltered for a moment, as if she had finally come to the part of the story she was not willing to share.

There was a noise as something small broke through the invisibility veil, and a black tom cat trotted along the balcony, making directly for Mneme.

Thornbury hissed between his teeth. "Edmund."

Not a cat at all, Mneme realised as she gazed into the creature's blinding moonlight eyes. No, this was a shape of shadow and magic. A memory of a person who once held incredible power, twisted into something domestic.

"Weren't you bigger when we met?" she asked softly.

Muscles flexed under shining black fur. The creature billowed and expanded into a monstrous form, half cat and half man, all shadow. Gently, he laid his head in Mneme's lap.

"Electra," Thornbury murmured.

"Don't you dare judge me, Thornbury. You did this to Edmund in the first place. You failed him."

"We failed him," Thornbury corrected. "He started a magical experiment that went horribly wrong, and his entire team failed to save him from the consequences. You were on that team as much as I was, Electra."

"He always relied on you to feed his magic when he over-extended himself…"

"And what have you done to him all these years? He should have drifted by now, crossed over to wherever it is magisters go when they die. But you kept him here, on a leash. He's the portable magic pocket, isn't he? That's why it kept moving around the island. You've been bleeding his magic for years, and for what? To build a gazebo for the Queen? To pull conjuring tricks out of your sleeve? To hide up here in the hills, keeping your tea hot? This was a one room workshop when we began, and you used his magic to build yourself a bloody manor house?"

"Don't you dare judge me," Electra yelled at him. "I'm trying to keep my family safe."

"If that's true," said Lady Persimmon. "Then *why* did you let us believe you were dead?"

The cat creature purred under Mneme's hand. Magic was already warming her veins, thanks to the pocket in which they breakfasted. But here, in proximity to this lovely creature, she felt her magic blossom. His power felt chaotic, jagged under her fingertips. As she stretched her own magic to meet his, she found the end of it, and sighed deeply. How very sad. "I expect you had the spell prepared ahead of time," she said in a conversational voice.

"What would you know about it?" Electra snapped.

"I can feel it. His magic is failing."

Thornbury's eyes went to her, and to the shadow-shape in her lap. He looked miserable. "Edmund?"

"You've been using his magic," Mneme said to Electra. "You must know he's at breaking point."

Electra hesitated, and then bowed her head. "We built this house together. A safe house. I had to do something. His magic was — I could feel it getting wilder. Bigger. I thought we needed to siphon it off, to calm him down. That perhaps if we used enough of his magic, he might be himself again."

Persimmon set her cup down with a clatter.

Electra turned to her again. "Not to save our marriage, you dolt. Believe me, if I managed to bring him back, I would divorce him in an instant. But I've always felt so guilty about how I lost him. About moving on, and finding love. I thought I was doing the right thing. But —" She pulled a face. "Mrs Seabourne is right. Using more of his magic made things worse. Things began to appear and disappear. The gazebo turned up in the Palace grounds one day by sheer accident — I managed to convince the Queen it was a clever gift and not a horrifying symptom of wild magic gone rogue."

She bowed her head. "I promised myself I wouldn't use his magic any more, after that. But once I realised I had to disappear, to fake my own death… I couldn't see a way to do it without magic."

"The spell went off early," Mneme guessed. "And it wasn't supposed to happen on some remote lake path. You would have wanted it to be near a magical pocket, so it made more sense."

Electra nodded. "I was going to have it happen at the masque, so the children would all be safely tucked into their beds at Manticore Manor. Persimmon, you would have known about it ahead of time, and you would be right there, able to claim custody rights as godmother." Her voice broke a little. "The Queen been waiting her entire reign for you to ask her for a favour, so she can feel a little less guilty about loving your husband. I could have hidden out here until it all blew over, and then made my way to Manticore. Set up a private home somewhere nearby, so you and the boys could visit me regularly."

Persimmon gave her a sad smile. "It was a good plan."

"It was a terrible plan," said Thornbury sharply. "You really thought Swift would have no interest in claiming his property?"

"He has no claim over my son," Electra said flatly. "This part is all your fault, Thornbury, don't talk to me."

Thornbury threw up both of his hands. "How is this mess anything to do with me?"

"You and your splendid marriage," Electra said furiously. She made a rude gesture in Mneme's direction. "In with the famous Seabournes now, on the up and up."

"My father has no love for my decision to marry," said Thornbury.

"Oh, you think so? Or did he convince you he disapproved because he doesn't like to reveal weakness? Believe me, he adores that you're one of the nobility now. He's bursting with pride that his grandchildren will all be red-headed Seabournes, and I daresay looking forward to manipulating every single one of them long before they come of age."

Thornbury looked quite ill at the thought of it.

"He told me that he would be taking Ed," said Persimmon in a quiet voice. "I believe he had in mind to hand him to the two of you, until he was of age to go to school…"

Mneme blinked. "Of course it would not occur to him to ask what we thought of the matter."

"And the whole cycle would start again," said Electra bitterly. "Another Swift to add to his legacy of cold-blooded spies."

"And what's your excuse for being cold-blooded?" Thornbury snapped back. "If the Queen is so keen to grant Lady Persimmon a favour, did neither of you consider that she can also grant royal decree divorces? The two of you could be married by now, and her Majesty might finally put everyone out of their misery and solve the diplomatic question of the decade by marrying the one man everyone knows that she wants."

Mneme found herself catching a breath. It was the most scandalous thing her husband had ever dared say aloud.

Electra laughed hollowly. "Ever the diplomat," she said to Thornbury. "The Queen has to marry a foreign prince, everyone knows that. And Lord Manticore needs to be married to *someone*, so that the Queen is available to marry a foreign prince."

"Yes," said Thornbury impatiently. "Fine. But he doesn't need to be married to you, Lady Persimmon. Surely some happiness is still possible."

Electra huffed, but the fight had gone out of her. "He wasn't ever this much of a romantic, Mrs Seabourne. Have you totally ruined him?"

"Oh," said Mneme. "I do hope so."

Thornbury gave her an impatient look, half loving and half irritated. Of his many expressions, it was one of her favourites.

The shadow creature on Mneme's lap shimmered again, and became more comfortably cat-shaped. She scratched him behind the ears. Magic was a heady taste after so long without it; she felt as if she had been drinking champagne with breakfast. "I think Mr Cheshire would like us to break his spell now," she observed.

Electra gave her a wild look. "Can you … do you think you can? I thought it was impossible."

"My wife is exceptionally talented," said Thornbury warmly.

"Yes, yes. Your friends must find you utterly sickening."

"They do," Mneme agreed absently, scratching Mr Cheshire's fur. "Thornbury, dear, how is your magic?"

"Recovered," he said. "Mneme, are you sure?"

Mr Cheshire's eyes burned green.

"He's unstable," she said. "He's fragmenting. It will happen soon, with or without us. This way, we might prevent a disaster." Power rippled under Mneme's fingers. "Can you feel that?" she asked Thornbury. "All the magical pockets… they do feel more like cracks now."

He nodded, troubled. "They're connected."

A roil of magic poured off Mr Cheshire, flooding Mneme's senses. She felt no longer champagne-tipsy with the power, but brandy-drunk. No wonder Electra had kept coming up with excuses to use her husband's residual magic; it was addictive, to be this powerful. "The tea room, the poetry library… the cracks are getting bigger."

"And out we go!" Thornbury stood, and Electra and Persimmon stood with him. "Can't be sure the house will stay standing, if we break the original spell. Mneme, can you let go of him?"

"I'm not sure." Mneme's hands were warm, laid upon the head of the doleful creature leaking magic into her and the surrounding house. "He's so tired."

Thornbury went down on one knee, catching the moonlight eyes of the shadow creature. "Time's up, old chum," he said, regret in his voice. "Here we go."

The creature's eyes glowed brighter and brighter: moonlight in the sunlit morning.

"You pushed me out of the way of a murderer last night," Mneme reminded him. "Thank you for that. You really have been watching over everyone, all this time, haven't you? Trying to keep an eye on things. It's all right, now. Job's done."

Gently, she kissed the shadow creature on the top of his head, then lifted him into her arms, took her husband's hand and moved away, off the balcony.

Electra and Persimmon were ahead of them, standing on the grass outside the invisibility field which flickered on and off. They were holding hands. Mneme placed Mr Cheshire carefully on the ground, and allowed herself to fall into the magic.

She was dimly aware of Thornbury, moving carefully around her, snipping threads of the complex tangle of wild magic. She loved to watch him work. This was different to his usual routine because there wasn't a single spell or even a formal network of spells to unravel.

Mr Cheshire's magic was wrapped up in the original shield spell over the whole Isle of Aster, and tangled in every crack in that spell, not to mention every shadow and crack and tendril that had emerged from that magic in the intervening years.

Mneme's own magic flared up, illuminating the darkness like moonlight in a room full of messy theatrical arte-facts. She lifted, untangled and smoothed the mess of wild magic emanating from Mr Cheshire and the island, as her husband severed the threads.

Finally, entropy took over. The magic slithered apart in whole matted chunks instead of individual threads. It was failing, failing faster than could possibly be controlled.

For a moment all of them saw a glowing figure: a pale man in glasses, concentrating hard. A ghost from the past. He said: "I think if we... I can just... break it."

The shield shattered.

The spell cracked.

"Done it!" shouted the pale man in triumph, and promptly disappeared in a shiver of light.

"Done it," Thornbury murmured under his breath, holding up a hand to bid farewell to his old friend.

The four of them stood together on the hillside, watching as magic returned to the Isle of Aster. Colours rose and fell: the sky boiled. It rained green and silver, for a while, with raindrops that tasted of elderflower cordial. And then...

Mneme breathed the thoroughly magical air into her lungs. "Her Majesty is going to need a report."

"I don't work for her," said Lady Persimmon, imme-diately.

"I'm legally dead," said Lady Cheshire, turning her face away so no one could see whether or not she was wiping a tear at witnessing the final end of her husband.

Mr C. Thornbury Seabourne sighed. "Duty first," he agreed, shooting a slightly guilty look at his wife.

Mneme laid her head on his shoulder. "I knew it when I married you," she reminded him.

HONEYMOON CONCLUDED, AND
FURTHER CORRESPONDENCE

*B*umbleton Palace was in an uproar when they returned. For the first time in generations, the palace was awash with magic.

Roses bloomed from the staircases, bread and butter-flies swarmed in the kitchen, and the portraits were furiously arguing with each other, returning to grudges more than a century old.

There had been an entire murder investigation while they were gone; and for once, Mneme and Thornbury had missed it.

"You'll never guess," said Juno, pouncing on them as they made their way towards the Queen's receiving parlour. "It was Great Aunt Edith who tried to kill Lord Manticore!"

"Really?" said Mneme, managing a spark of interest despite being exhausted from a night of no sleep, far too much worry, a magical power-boost and two hill-hikes. The hem of her midnight fairy gown was wet with dew.

And yet, a murder investigation had taken place in their absence.

"We solved it," Juno said with glee. "Me and Henry. Just like you and Thornbury usually do. We called all the suspects together and made several terribly wrong accusations, and just as the Queen was about to lose her temper and banish us from the Teacup Isles forever, Henry produced a white wig-hair from inside the second unicorn head, and I figured out her motivations and basically, we're both terribly clever. I think I might marry him, you know."

"Seems like a good investment," said Mneme with a weak smile. "Why on earth was Great Aunt Edith out to murder Lord Manticore?"

"Oh, you know," Juno said airily. "The scandal no one ever discusses in public. She thought she was saving the Queen from hurling herself at a married man, or some balderdash. Good thing she was so terrible at murder or we'd have a dead Lord on our hands. Now, what have you two been up to? You're not behind this sudden magical revival, are you? The cooks are livid." She glanced around at their party just in time to see Lady Persimmon and Mrs Cheshire disappear through the doors with the bronze lions, to meet with the Queen. "Isn't one of those ladies supposed to be dead?"

"It's a long story," said Mneme, patting Juno on the arm.

Thornbury hesitated on the threshold, and then pulled the doors closed without stepping through. He turned back to Mneme. "I think perhaps we'll leave them to it, don't you? Let someone else make the report for a change."

"You know Electra will blame you for everything," Mneme warned him.

"I'll risk it. This is supposed to be my honeymoon."

"You can have breakfast with us and tell us everything," said Juno delighted.

Mneme gave a heavy sigh. "A small breakfast," she

agreed. "And several cups of tea. After that, I'm taking my husband home. It has been a very long night indeed."

❧

MR AND MRS SEABOURNE returned to Comfrey Cottage by palace carriage drawn by actual horses, which was something of a miracle considering that the palace stables were currently overrun by magical creatures that were definitely not horses. They were lucky not to end up with something purple and bat-winged.

Having been repressed of magic for so many years, the Isle of Aster was rather overdoing it.

"I'm sorry," Mneme said, as the carriage drew up in front of their honeymoon home. The village pub they had passed on the way was clearly suffering from unexpectedly-floating barrels, dancing tankards and locals who had found themselves speaking all manner of unfamiliar languages including one that had previously only been understood by elves.

Comfrey Cottage, by comparison, looked relatively normal, but she had no idea what would await them within.

"What on earth for?" asked her husband, stepping down from the carriage and extending a hand to assist her with her heavy skirts.

"You were so enjoying our sojourn in Aster. When you weren't secretly hunting rogue magic in the hills. Now the shield is finally broken for good, you've lost any chance of escape from the magical world." There had been a lightness to Thornbury over the past few weeks that she had never seen in him before, a bone-deep happiness.

Thornbury made a gentle chuffing noise. "I did marry

recently, you know," he chided her, as he unlatched the front door and hustled her over the threshold.

"I heard a rumour to that effect." Mneme suspected what he was going to say next, and her mouth formed a gentle smile in anticipation.

"Do you not think that acquiring a splendid wife is enough reason to enjoy my *escape*, as you put it, regardless of whether there's magic in the air?"

"I suppose…"

Thornbury tipped up her chin and kissed her lightly. "You are a fool if you think otherwise, Mnemosyne. And I know you to be no fool."

She took a deep breath and let it out, quite slowly. "I want to go home," she sighed.

Given that where they were standing, there could be no confusion about what she meant. Thornbury, a little distracted with tidying the stray coils of hair from her neck, stilled for a moment. "Truly home? Henry says it will be a few weeks yet before the manse all finished and ready for us to move in."

Sleepy and comfortable, Mneme leaned heavily into him. "*Home*," she breathed dreamily.

"You wish to live among carpenters and drop cloths?"

"I do," she said fiercely, clutching at his shirt sleeves. "I want to begin our real life together. Properly."

"And you realise it will be … more of this sort of thing." He gave a vague wave to the garden, clearly implying the chaos they had witnessed in the village and the palace. *Magical disasters and cut-throat politics.* "Pretty much for the rest of our lives."

"Oh, I do hope so, Mr Seabourne," she said meaningfully.

"Well, then," said Thornbury, looking rather pleased. "As you say, Mrs Seabourne. Let us pack for home."

Mneme shook her head, tangled her fingers in his, and led him to the staircase. "Bed, Mr Seabourne. Sleep. Then packing. Then home. The secret to a successful marriage is to always observe the proper order of things."

"And to accept that my wife knows best in all things."

"That, my dear, goes without saying."

~

FROM: *JUNO, DUCHESS OF STORM, STILL HAPPILY ENSCONCED IN THE GUEST APARTMENTS AT BUMBLETON PALACE, WHERE ALL THE BEST GOSSIP IS TO BE HAD*

TO: *MRS M. SEABOURNE AT THE HARE AND WICKET, NORTH VILLAGE, THE ISLE OF STORM*

My dear, such news!!!

I can't believe you've tucked yourself off home to supervise a bunch of carpenters and wall-painters who surely have a better idea than you about what needs to be done. Only to stay in a public house in the village of all things, because of course your new home does not have carpets yet.

You could be here with me, learning everything first-hand, as an entire island discovers how to manage its own magic all over again!

Who would have thought shabby old Bumbleton was the place to be this summer, instead of Town and Court?

And oh, where to start?

First, the scandalous separation is no longer a mere rumour. Lord and Lady M have formally petitioned the

Queen for divorce, as the Court of Lords and Parliament of Gentles are both closed for the summer.

I've never seen Lady P (she won't be Lady M for much longer) smile so much as in the last few days, and her husband looks mightily delighted also. In public they are the best of friends, as if ending their marriage has made them entirely better disposed towards each other. It's a kindness for the children, I suppose, to settle things in an amicable fashion, but the aunties are all greatly concerned it will start a fashion for severing unwanted marriages.

As for Great Aunt E, it's as if she never existed, so thoroughly disgraced that no one will even speak her name. The dreadful donkey head has been returned to the Moonlight Gallery, and Lord M has declared he wants the informational plaque updated to include his dramatic near-death experience.

Then there's Mrs C, sinister feline that she is. Somehow she has everyone who is anyone purring in the palm of her hand, claiming credit as she has (in equal part with her deceased husband, at least) for the return of magic to the Isle of Aster. I'm not sure she's won friends and influenced people among the ordinary folk, who have had to radically change their tourism brand, but at least we can all get a piping hot cup of tea at the proper temperature whenever we like.

Anyway, Mrs C (whose miraculous return from the dead is rumoured to be part of her marvellous spell-cracking achievement or some tosh like that) is the toast of the palace, *despite* her recent resignation from the Queen's service, and no one is even slightly impressed that Henry and I solved an attempted murder on the same night.

Ay me, I might as well come home myself at this rate — at least then I could host you and Thornbury if you do insist on hovering around your home before it's properly habitable.

Except, of course, that every time Henry suggests we make a move, something even more interesting happens, and I can't bear to miss a moment of it!

Your friend,
Juno

~

FROM: *C. THORNBURY SEABOURNE*

TO: *OCTAVIAN SWIFT, QUEEN'S CONSULTANT - WISTWORIA PALACE, THE ISLE OF TOWN*

Sir,

I am sure that your other agents have kept you apprised of the matter of Aster, and the return of magic to this isle.

I wished to update you on a legal situation arising from the complex situation. Mr Edmund Bedford Cheshire, previously reported to have died during the second summer of Queen Aud's reign, had in fact remained living until recent events, continuing to investigate the magical challenge set for him by palace officials. His recent death, in finishing his work, was witnessed by myself, my wife, and two others. Our signed statements to this effect have been processed by the local constabulary, with Mr Cheshire's personal information revised.

This means, as I am sure you are aware, that there can be no question as to the parentage of Edmund Alfred Cheshire, son of the above. I believe that his mother, whose recent death was also falsely reported, has nominated the boy's godmother as his guardian in the event of her next death.

Any attempt to circumvent this particular legal situation would be, as far as I am concerned, a final straw as to whether or not I am prepared to offer my services to your department in future.

Yours sincerely,
Thornbury

～

FROM: *OCTAVIAN SWIFT, QUEEN'S CONSULTANT, WISTWORIA PALACE, THE ISLE OF TOWN*

TO: *C. THORNBURY SEABOURNE, C/O THE HARE AND WICKET, NORTH VILLAGE, THE ISLE OF STORM*

My dear Charles

I have, of course, no idea as to why you think the parentage of the Cheshire boy is any concern of mine.

But your point is made.

Do send my regards to your wife.

Swift

～

FROM: *LADY PERSIMMON MANTICORE, YARROW VILLA, THE ISLE OF ASTER*

TO: *MRS M. SEABOURNE, TEMPEST MANSE, NORTH VILLAGE, THE ISLE OF STORM*

Dear Mnemosyne,

I never had a chance to thank you and your husband for your part in the affairs of last summer, which have eventuated in such a welcome outcome for myself and my family.

The children and I have moved our permanent residence to our lakeside villa near Mudgely for now, as it is most convenient for them to see their father when he is in the country. On the rare occasions that he is at home, I have the Dower House at my disposal, and Lord Manticore has assured me this will be the case even after the divorce is decreed. It is quite enough space for us and all the nursemaids, as the Manticore ancestors had a tendency towards the unnecessarily large.

I suspect, sooner or later, Lord M will give up the 'big house' altogether except for occasional holidays and public events, which might be for the best. I spent so many years rattling around in it, and it never felt particularly like a home.

As summer gives way to autumn, I am looking forward to a new future, and the enclosed invitation may give you a clue as to what that future entails.

Electra and I will be married in winter, on the Isle of Sensibility, with our family and some friends in attendance. I hope you and Mr Seabourne will be free to join us, along with Inspector and Mrs Holiday. The resort we have chosen is quite accessible by portal.

My future wife is considering new professional opportunities, as she felt that a withdrawal from the Queen's service was necessary to avoid the political troubles that endangered our family. She has received several offers, thanks to the public acclaim she received for reviving the magics of the Isle of Aster, and may well accept a lecturing position at Delphi College in the new year.

Please pass on to your husband my appreciation for the letter he wrote to a mutual acquaintance last month, as I know that Electra will never quite bring herself to thank him herself.

Warm regards,
The future Mrs Persimmon Melusine

∾

EXCERPT FROM LETTERS TO THE EDITOR, *THE GENTLEWOMAN*

> I greatly enjoyed the interview with the Queen about her new shepherdess fashion, and every girl in my village is now sporting pink and white ribbons! But why-oh-why did Miss Wheaten not ask the question that simply everyone wants to know: when will the Queen give us a royal wedding?
>
> Surely there's at least one prince on the Continent who will win her favour? Or perhaps a gentleman closer to home?

> EDITOR'S NOTE: *any letter which includes the legal name of a prospective or rumoured suitor for the Queen's hand will not be published in this magazine.*

∾

PRIVATE NOTES DELIVERED BY INGENIOUS NON-MAGICAL
DEVICE, TEMPEST MANSE, NORTH VILLAGE, ISLE OF
STORM

HUSBAND,

Our new home is full of such marvels and surprises.
Imagine my joy to find a note-flinging contraption in the
drawer of my dressing table!

Remember we have interviews for household staff at
three. But absolutely no appointments for the next three
hours

Yours,
Mrs Seabourne

~

WIFE,

Is that a hint? To bring you tea and cake in our new
library, perhaps?
Mr Seabourne

~

HUSBAND,

I will not complain if you bring tea and cake, but I am
certainly not in the library.

More to the point, if you do not appear in our
bedroom in the next ten minutes, I shall have to put my
nightgown back on.

M.

~

PRIVATE NOTE DELIVERED BY MAGICAL PAPER BIRD TO THE MASTER SUITE OF TEMPEST MANSE, NORTH VILLAGE, ISLE OF STORM

MY DARLING WIFE,

I would join you in the bedroom, but I'm afraid I have strayed into a patch of sunshine in the garden, and made myself very comfortable.

Come and find me.

Mr S.

THE END

GLOSSARY OF THE TEACUP ISLES
HONEYMOON EDITION

- Aster, Isle of — a minor island within the Lordship of Manticore, famous for its lack of magic, its splendid holiday lake and its country ways
- Bath, Isle of — one of the Teacup Isles: a holiday destination with healing waters
- Bumbleton Palace — the Queen's country palace, on the minor Isle of Aster
- Continent, the — an extremely large island, beyond the Lyric Sea, foreign but fashionable
- Croquet, the new — a jolly game involving young ladies, sticks, balls and creative sorcery
- Court of Lords, the — one of the two official government bodies of the Teacup Isles; the aristocratic one
- Curricle — a two-wheeled carriage driven with two horses; no footmen required
- Delphi College — a magical university, mostly reserved for the very wealthy (and a small number of scholarship students)

- Dormouse, Isle of — one of the Teacup Isles: a barony and a source of rather good tea
- Gentlewoman, the — a lady's magazine full of fashion plates, cosmetic recipes and discreet employment advertisements
- Ices — a delicious frozen dessert made from flavoured custards and cordials; terribly expensive in summer, and really quite reasonably priced in winter
- Luncheon — a light midday meal often enjoyed by ladies, and occasionally hijacked by gentlemen
- Lyric Sea, the — home to the Teacup Isles
- Madeleines — tiny curved sponge cakes, baked in cast iron moulds with a specific shell-like design
- Magisters — mysterious working magicians, blamed and/or credited for all manner of sinister goings on
- Manticore, Isle of — one of the Teacup Isles: a lordship
- Manse — a house provided for the senior temple priest or magister of a town or village, and their family
- Masque — a costume ball in which all participants are expected to be masked
- Memory, Isle of — one of the Teacup Isles: quiet, peaceful
- Midsummer Night's Occurrence — a popular tragic play by Sir Dilles Blightweather, about the Midnight Fairy, tricked into loving a mortal with the head of a donkey. Everyone dies at the end, except the donkey.
- Mudgely — a lakeside village on the Isle of

Aster, within walking distance of Bumbleton Palace

- Muslin — the lightest possible of cotton fabric, very fashionable and worn by ladies in pale white and cream colours
- Name day — far more important than birthdays, with better presents
- Parliament of Gentles, the — one of the two official government bodies of the Teacup Isles; the slightly more egalitarian one
- Portals — a magical method of stepping through magical gateways. Restricted to male use until very recently, thanks to a revolutionary campaign led by a certain Miss Mnemosyne Seabourne
- Queen of Hearts — a comic opera about a tyrannical queen who executes all her husbands
- Ratafia — a fortified wine, flavoured with almond, spice or orange blossom; or, in a pinch, any fruity punch that is also alcoholic
- Sandwich, Isle of — one of the Teacup Isles: an earldom
- Season — that part of the year when unmarried nobility are positively encouraged to court each other in dramatic fashion: begins with the opening of the Court of Lords at the end of autumn, continues with the opening of the Parliament of Gentles in midwinter, and can be extended by garden parties and house parties well into spring if your mamma is steadfast enough
- Sensibility, the Isle of — one of the Teacup Isles: a duchy. The first isle to legalise same sex marriage and adoption

- Shellwich Standing — the Seabourne family home, on the isle of Memory
- Spellcracker — a professional person whose specialty is the removal, shielding and dissolving of unwanted magics
- Storm, Isle of — one of the Teacup Isles: a dukedom.
- Storm Bolt — the Duke of Storm's townhouse, featuring four secret passages, twelve maids, three libraries and the best of all possible butlers
- Storm North — the Duke of Storm's country seat
- Swan-shaped boats — once the only polite manner of travel between islands for those of the female persuasion; now desperately old-fashioned
- Sympathetic magic — a minor form of spellcraft, using objects (often charmed) to form small but significant shifts in reality, will or marital status
- Tempest Manse — a newly built home for the Duke of Storm's spellcracker, and his wife
- Town, Isle of — the centre of most social activity in the Teacup Isles, featuring the Isle of Court
- Wistworia Palace — a palace in Town

ABOUT THE AUTHOR

Tansy Rayner Roberts is an award-winning Australian science fiction and fantasy author who never wears corsets or muslin. She lives with her family in Tasmania and has been known to pick up the occasional embroidery hoop.

- Listen to Tansy on Sheep Might Fly, a podcast where she reads aloud her stories as audio serials.
- Read some of Tansy's stories before anyone else when you pledge to her Patreon: patreon.com/tansyrr
- What tea is Tansy drinking? Find out at: tinyurl. com/tansyrr when you subscribe to her excellent newsletter.

ALSO BY TANSY RAYNER ROBERTS

Tea & Sympathetic Magic

There's nothing more dangerous than an eligible duke...

Every eligible young lady of the Teacup Isles wants to marry the Duke of Storm, except Miss Mnemosyne Seabourne, who is quite content on the shelf, thank you very much. All she wants is a quiet life and a good book.

At a house party full of ruthless debutantes willing to employ sneaky sympathetic magic to win a husband of quality, Mneme joins forces with an enigmatic spellcracker to rescue the duke from being married against his will.

Can Mneme save the Duke of Storm without becoming his bride? Will this caper ruin her reputation forever? Can teacups and hedgehogs be used as projectile weapons in emergencies? Why are attractive men more devastating when they roll up their sleeves?

If you enjoy Regency house parties, witty romantic banter and high society sorcery, you'll adore this magical comedy of manners cosy mystery novella.

The Frost Fair Affair

Our heroine stumbles across a precarious plot while printing political pamphlets...

Thanks to last Season's scandal involving her family, Miss Mnemosyne Seabourne is officially notorious. Wintering in Town, she hopes to use her new celebrity to campaign about the unfair restriction on portal travel for ladies… while being quietly courted by a certain handsome spellcracker.

As the river freezes over and a spectacular Frost Fair sets up on the ice, Mneme finds herself beset by secret societies, spies and sneaky saboteurs. Who stole her political pamphlets? Who is leaving dead bodies around printing presses for anyone to find?

Mr Thornbury knows more than he's letting on. If she can't trust the man she hoped to marry, Mneme is just going to have to unravel the mystery for herself, quick enough to save both of their lives.

If you enjoy vintage spy adventures, flirtatious couples and cosy sleigh rides, you'll adore this exciting sequel novella to *Tea and Sympathetic Magic*.

Castle Charming

In this fairy tale kingdom, the royals of Castle Charming have always been cursed. What will it take to heal their family, and survive the magical threat overwhelming their land?

The cruel truth behind fairy godmothers.

Disaster princes cursed to dance all night.

A sleeping spell with a taste for royal blood.

A giant attack beanstalk.

A powerful magical princess who could destroy them all.

Castle Charming is an enormously fun collection of LGBTQ+ fairy tale adventure novellas.

CPSIA information can be obtained
at www.ICGtesting.com
Printed in the USA
LVHW040956160721
692882LV00025B/2026

9 780648 898337